WILD BREED

WILD BREED

TED STRATTON

CUTTING EDGE

ISBN-13: 978-1-962896-90-0

Published by
Cutting Edge Books
PO Box 8212
Calabasas, CA 91372
www.cuttingedgebooks.com

CHAPTER ONE

WITHIN THE FASTNESSES of the Ramapo Mountains, the York State land lay green and brown and bare at early-morning sun. Above the cupped meadow, a cabin and barn and outbuildings stood on level ground. The cabin had a huge chimney, steeply pitched roof, tar paper tight over the siding, windows except to the north, and dirt banked high at the foundation line. In the stillness, the south door opened.

Into April, bareheaded Stewart Yeoman stepped, wearing a blue shirt, clean denims, and work shoes. Ignoring the backhouse, with a sickle moon carved in the door, he performed a ritual to greet the new day. He wet down the back yard.

Noting the scant wood supply in the attached shed, he knew that Brother John, a loafer, never would cut and carry maple for Gran's cookstove, and knew also that the old man might not do it, either. He would have done the chore himself, but there was a log cabin to build for Mrs. McCaffrey, who lived with her husband in a great stone house on the Valley road.

Everywhere, spring advanced into the hills. On the stark thrust of Lonesome Ridge, shadbush spattered vague whiteness against the building hardwoods. Here the meadow turned green and grackles clamored at the brook, where a man might catch a panful of brown trout if Corbett, the game warden, wasn't around to snoop.

"Promises a good day," Stewart decided, rubbing a freshly shaved face. "Sun'll shine on both sides of the fence."

Then he remembered that the old man and John, who had gadded off to gun a deer yesterday afternoon, hadn't come roaring home in the middle of the night to brag about fresh mountain "beef" and to hell with Corbett's law. Probably the men had failed to bag that deer and had camped in the woods for an early start this morning.

Down by the curling road, movement caught Stewart's attention. Nelda, John's wife from the Valley, left a tumbled cabin and entered the meadow. She wore a short dress and swung a dip bucket. At every high step in the dewy grass, Nelda busted a rainbow and flashed bare legs. Stewart's breath plumed faster.

What was in John's blood that he wandered the woods and there was better sport at home?

In one hand Stewart carried two willow whistles that he had carved for John's sons, Tad and Ned. The way John neglected the boys, they didn't have much, but they'd find a pile of fun in the whistles. Suddenly his face darkened.

Within a tangle of staghorn sumac and white birch a furlong distant, a huge man left a partially hidden cabin and strode to the fence line. The newcomer was Caleb Hall. As if he owned Yeoman land, Caleb slid backside over the top rail and toted a bucket down to the spring hole that fed the meadow.

If that Valley man fusses with Nelda, Stewart thought, I'll kick his behind onto his shoulders.

At the spring, man and woman met. When Nelda stooped to dip her bucket, Caleb grabbed her wrist. For a moment they stood close together, arm touching arm, leg brushing leg; then Caleb filled Nelda's bucket with sweet mountain water.

That is wrong, Stewart thought, for a true wedded wife to lollygag first thing in the morning. Besides, it was a woman's chore to dip and fetch her man's water.

When Nelda turned, she spotted Stewart in the back yard and called up: "John home yet?"

"Ain't seen him," Stewart answered.

"Your father?"

"Ain't seen him, neither."

"What keeps them so long in the woods?"

"Must like it there."

"Stewart, when will they come home?"

"Can't rightly figure."

"Will you come here, please?"

Stewart strode off.

Barely twenty-one, he had wide shoulders and quick muscles to heft an oak log, thick wrists and strong fingers that knew how to power an ax or gentle a rifle. At the moment, his dark hawk's eyes were neither soft nor predatory, merely watchful. Straight black hair slicked his head. The nostrils of his Roman nose flared. His skin wore the cast of a tarnished penny. In those external characteristics, Stewart resembled all Yeomans.

Long ago inside this virgin wilderness, a Yeoman had courted an Indian maid one witch-moon night, fetching her home as wife. As the wolves had howled on Lonesome Ridge and the varmints had caterwauled from the hollows, Delaware blood had crossed with English immigrant stock. It was this Indian heritage that had self-taught Stewart to walk with a peculiar bent-kneed, toed-in, effortless shuffle.

At the spring, he handed the whistles to Nelda. "Saw some willow sweating," he explained shyly, "and carved 'em. Guess the sons can have a pile of fun now."

"That was kind of you, Stewart."

Nelda had been reared on a farm down the Sloatsburg road, which made her a Valley girl. She was a Starr and wore her mother's look. Her eyes were blue, her skin was tanned, her hair gold as a dandelion, and her lips were the red of wild strawberries.

"I keep worrying about the men," Nelda said. "What keeps them so long on the trail?"

Standing so close to Nelda, Stewart sensed hot blood course up his spine and thicken his thinking. Self-consciously, his eyes lowered. "I see no cause to fret," he told Nelda's wet shoes. "Men don't mind a night in the woods."

Caleb drawled: "They went deer huntin'?"

There was no shyness in the way that Stewart wheeled to Caleb and waited for the man to speak again.

"I drunk beer in the Valley yesterday," Caleb added. "Yeomans went huntin' illegal?"

Stewart said shortly: "It's our born right to hunt any time we see the need."

"That ain't what Warden Corbett thinks. I heard he caught John once with fresh venison and got John fined fifty bucks. I heard they had a fist fight, too."

Nelda said: "They only had words."

"Hot words head to a ruckus," Caleb said, smacking his lips. "I heard John swore to fix Corbett good. Fists or guns, John bragged. Corbett said he was always ready. That the truth of it, Stewart?"

Stewart measured Caleb, who had small eyes and a vast nose. Caleb stood four inches taller and he had longer arms and thicker hips, plus a forty-pound weight advantage. Also, he had been around longer and was seven years older.

"For a long spell," Stewart said carefully, "you been off this hill. In the month you been back at your old man's place, you heard too much rumor. One thing is true: Be it guns or fists, John can settle Corbett."

"That Hill brag?"

"True fact. Corbett's a Valley man."

"I was downhill yesterday," Caleb continued. "Nauright at the Black Bear Inn wants fresh venison. Nauright asked did I know a hunter and I mentioned Yeomans."

"Tell Nauright to gun his own meat."

"He promised thirty dollars for a dressed carcass. If John takes the job, he can buy dainties for pretty Nelda." Caleb eyed the silent woman. "You like a new dress?"

Nelda wore a faded dress. It fitted her body so tightly that the neckline popped the upper curves of her breasts into view. "I guess," she murmured, "a Valley girl soon learns the simple, hard life on the Hill. My mother always said a daughter marries for better or worse and must make the best of her lot. The fact is I am rich with young Tad and little Ned around."

Because he did not like the way Caleb stared at Nelda's breasts, Stewart blurted: "Ain't nobody 'cept Corbett to keep you from earnin' Nauright's dirty dollars."

"It ain't Corbett and his law that stops me from huntin'," Caleb bragged, swelling his huge muscles for Nelda to admire. "By God, I ain't seen no tinhorn on this hill I can't tame, neither! If I needed cash like John Yeoman does, I'd gun a deer for Nauright! If I owned a rifle, and I don't, I'd kill a buck!"

"Maybe," Stewart said slyly, "you are smart enough to scare a buck to death."

Nelda said quickly: "Stew-art dear, is Gran worried about the men out so long?"

"Gran slept good."

"Will the men be home for breakfast victuals?"

"Should be."

"If they don't come soon?"

"No cause to fret, Nelda. If the men didn't bag a buck last night, they will try today. Sunrise and sunset is the best time for deer and the men know that."

Nelda persisted: "Where did they plan to hunt?"

"Can't rightly say. Gran told me the men just whistled the dog and lit off."

"Yesterday," Caleb said, "I was in the Valley. Come to remember, I heard shooting as I walked up the Hill road just afore dark." Caleb spat tobacco juice on the grass and Stewart stiffened. "That might have been the Yeomans bangin' at a deer. Might have been the Mason tribe from across the lake. Masons ain't particular when they gun a deer, either."

Stewart demanded: "You heard how much shootin'?"

"Three-four shots."

"That warn't the old man and John. A Yeoman needs one shot to drop a buck." It pleased him to correct Caleb in front of Nelda. "Hill men ain't like Valley men, that fire a dozen shots to kill a sparrow. We ain't Valley bastards."

Caleb's mean eyes glinted. "You hint because I lived a time in the Valley I am a bastard?"

"Suit yourself. On the Hill, men don't sit on their backsides all day, neither."

Nelda interposed a smooth question between the angry men. "Stew-art, how long will you work at the McCaffreys'?"

"Each day, 'cept Sunday."

"Is young Mrs. McCaffrey so awful pretty?"

"I don't notice."

Caleb laughed. "Nelda, you can't expect a young sprout to know his way around a pretty woman."

Anger reddened the back of Stewart's neck. "By God," he said, "a lot of things I know and don't know. I do a man's work every day and that is more than some men can say. I don't spit on another man's meadow grass and I don't walk where I ain't wanted, neither. How's that for a peck of crab apples?"

That was a challenge.

Whatever stirred inside Caleb's mind failed to show on his face. He shrugged off the insults and glanced at Nelda. She picked up the full dip bucket.

Stewart growled, "That is my say for this morning," and, wheeling, he quick-stepped up the path. Through his angry mind paraded words his father had taught him.

Ever since Caleb's grandfather had drifted onto the Hill from Nyack way and settled that poor patch of ground on the knoll, there had been bad trouble between Yeoman and Hall. One day the greedy grandfather had dared stake out a claim on the rich meadowland, but a Yeoman gun had talked and crippled the grandfather. Years later, Caleb's father had hired a lawyer and summoned the Yeomans into court. In the Valley they had argued about true boundary lines, surveys, land grants, and rightful deeds, but the Yeomans had won that battle. When one bad Hall thing led to another, one day—Stewart was six years old—his father had run the Hall tribe off, and, until Caleb had sneaked back last month, no Hall had been seen on the Hill.

Pausing in the back yard, Stewart glanced below. Nelda neared John's cabin and Caleb headed through the tangle on Hall land. Under the rising sun, the meadow lay peaceful.

Why was Nelda worried about John out overnight? Everybody knew John cared more for hunting and applejack than he did about home. 'Twas a true fact that John didn't take care of Nelda and the sons the way a man should. Now, if he was married to Nelda…

Stewart entered the cabin.

CHAPTER TWO

I N THE LARGE MAIN ROOM, a gaunt fireplace, a window, and a rung ladder to the storage attic filled the west wall. At the north side, two doors studded a partition. One door led to Gran's room with the old man; the other to Stewart's bedroom. At the east side, faded cretonne curtains hid two wall bunks, one above the other, but no Yeoman slept there.

A woodbox flanked the hot cookstove. There were a hewn table, several chairs, a bench, and the old man's favorite sitting place, a barrel chair. Spare clothes decorated the walls. Stewart's rifle and shotgun rested on pegs, his ax and adze waited in a corner. Racks contained many chipped dishes and staples lined some shelves. Two frayed bearskins lay on the ancient puncheon floor. Not much else met the casual eye, but the Yeomans owned more than most Hill men.

Gran puttered at the stove.

She was a wispy woman, her thin body clothed in a soiled wraparound loose over a nightdress. Her face had a faraway, not-quite-here expression. That was because of George Yeoman. Straight as a whitewood sapling, George had been the tallest and eldest son. One tragic day behind Tamburn's general store at the crossroads, a power saw had busted loose and split George's skull into two pieces. The Yeomans had stowed George in a bury box, lugged him up to the orchard plot, and lowered him into a bury hole.

Now Gran whined: "That Valley woman was to the spring?"

"Nelda was there," Stewart said.

"She ain't no good for John!"

"Nelda's just different from our ways."

"Ain't no Valley woman wuth her salt, boy."

"Nelda has to put up with a lot, livin' with John in that leaky cabin and half the time no food for the sons 'cept the milk and staples we fetch down."

"Don't you say naught agin my man son John!" Gran shrilled. "That Valley woman ain't fit to slop the pig!" Gran banged a pan on the stove. "Boy, you seen my man?"

"No."

"You seen John?"

"No."

"What keeps 'em to the woods?"

"Guess they headed for New York town."

"It ain't a joke," Gran grumbled, dabbing at rheumy eyes. "I feel it in my bones somethin' bad has happened to the men. I feel just like the day George went off to work to Tamburn's store an' rode home feet fust on a pine board. I tole George not to go to work that day. Tole him I had the bad feelin' in my bones, but he went off an' died. Yesterday I tole the old man not to traipse after a buck. He went his own way." Gran sniffed. "A man don't never pay heed to his woman talkin' sense."

"Sure, sure," Stewart said soothingly, and sat at the table. "That potatoes aburnin'?"

"You et burnt 'taters afore. You stick up for that Valley woman an' I feed you naught but wind puddin'." Gran slopped victuals on Stewart's plate and padded to the south window. "Boy, I got the bad feelin' in my bones."

"Eat some food."

"Ain't been a mite hungry, not since George died."

Stewart wolfed a man's breakfast of burned potatoes, chunks of doughy oven bread, shriveled slices of pig's jowls, hot coffee cooled with milk and sweetened with store sugar. Finished, he said: "That was good victuals, Gran." Donning a cap and coat, he picked up a tin lunch pail and loaded his shoulders with ax and adze.

"Boy," Gran whined, "where you headin'?"

"To the McCaffreys'."

"You don't go to seek the men?"

"They are safe."

"Boy, you seek in the woods!"

Stewart frowned. "Gran, if one Yeoman was gone and not back, I'd turn the woods upside down. With two Yeomans together there is no cause for fret. Any second the men'll stomp home and their bellies starved."

"They ain't never stompin' home!"

"That is only a woman's fears," Stewart said kindly, and strode into the sun.

What fretted both women today? They fretted more than a hen with chicks, and not a hawk anywhere in the sky. He walked the rocky lane.

Soon the dogwood trees'd burst buds to snow the hills, and nothing was prettier than dogwood, white as Nelda's legs. No, Nelda's legs were tanned from the sun. Dogwood was like young Mrs. McCaffrey and her white skin that morning she stood at her back window, not wearing a stitch.

At John's cabin, young Tad and little Ned toddled forth. Tad was more than three years old, Ned almost two. Stewart set his things down, hoisted the sons high, and whirled them around. Their laughter fetched Nelda.

Nelda asked anxiously: "The men home?"

"No."

"They never stayed this long before."

Stewart swung the sons down and patted their heads. "I'll fetch some candy from Tamburn's store," he promised, and turned to Nelda. "They are fine sons."

She asked softly: "At the last scamper, why didn't you dance with me?"

"You had plenty o' partners."

"That's your reason?"

"Well—"

"Stew-art dear, are you afraid of me?"

He wanted to blurt, I loved you from the time I first set eyes on you afore John's wedding, but the words stuck fast in his throat. Because he dared not answer Nelda's question, he grabbed up his gear and legged down the curling road. Two blue jays scolded from an oak and a gray squirrel chattered angrily. By the north woods, smoke plumed from Red Scomp's chimney. At the Dunn place, old Pete tinkered with a topless car.

Stewart sang out: "That car run yit?"

"Goddanged car is stubborn," old Pete cackled, and swore a blue streak. "I don't want to traipse no place special, just like to hear the goddanged engine hum."

"Car run for you *once*."

"Ke-rist, that time she had wings!"

Stewart reached Tamburn's closed store at the crossroads and hit the Valley road. The sun turned warmer, as if spring were truly here. Minutes later, a green sedan approached, and Stewart stepped aside.

Warden Corbett stopped and leaned out the window. He had a weathered face and keen eyes under a peaked cap, and wore a gray shirt, green tie, silver badge, and holstered .38.

Corbett said: "Mornin', boy."

Stewart nodded.

"Last night, did you hear shooting back of the Hill?"

Stewart waited.

"You're sure full of talk this morning in April. Maybe you ate too much fresh venison for breakfast!" Corbett stared long. "Now, about that shooting I heard. It was before dark, about six-ten by my watch. At six-ten last night, where were your father and brother John?"

Stewart eyed a spiraling hawk.

"They hunted deer?"

The hawk drifted off.

"Say something, boy!"

Stewart said: "You are a Valley man."

Corbett leaned farther out the window. "I warned the Yeomans not to hunt deer in April and that's the state law. I warned the Yeomans not to gun after sunset and that's the state law." Corbett's eyes hardened. "When I heard those shots, I checked your place. Nelda was alone at John's cabin. You and Gran were home, but not the old man and John. What about that, boy?"

Stewart turned sideways and let the blunt ends of ax and adze drift past Corbett's chin. He asked softly: "You set foot on our place last night?"

"If the law is broken, I'll step where I like."

"You best remember there ain't a law agin shootin' a varmint an' I see one move in the bush."

"That a threat?"

"I don't look for trouble."

"Boy, you're too big for your Hill britches! Don't you talk big to me! If anybody shoots at a game warden, the Hill will crawl with state troopers!"

Stewart's shoulders moved. The keen blade of the ax slid around and missed Corbett's chin. Like a turtle ducking inside its shell, Corbett pulled his head in.

Stewart drawled, "I mind my business," and strode off.

Leaving the dusty road, Stewart took the short cut toward the ridge. His feet whispered pleasantly among the dead leaves. When he reached the crest, he walked a half mile to a cleared space where a square cabin frame, ten chestnut logs high, waited for roof timbers under a wolf pine. The south wall faced a cliff. That was so young Mrs. McCaffrey might sit at the window and gaze across the sweep of rough land, see the shine of a lonesome lake, and watch the thrust of a running ridge.

The sun said it was almost eight o'clock. Mr. McCaffrey had left the house for the automobile ride down to Haverstraw, where he owned a textile mill. Easing to the end of the knoll, Stewart joined the shadow of a pine tree.

There stretched the McCaffrey house, garage, and graveled back yard. The house had a blue-slate roof, stone sides filled with many leaded windows. Iron furniture, painted white, stood on flat rocks that young Mrs. McCaffrey called her pat-i-o. In the brook off, the side lawn she had gold fish. Well, not exactly *gold;* more red.

This morning, she didn't pose at the bedroom window. He remembered something that she was always saying. "After Mr. McCaffrey leaves for Haverstraw, I am alone upstairs. I always have a cup of coffee in bed. Why don't you join me?" That puzzled him. Did she mean join in the bed or in the coffee?

Why did a grown woman drink coffee in bed?

Shaking his head in puzzlement, he shouldered the ax, and, like a shadow, merged with the landscape.

The sun was June-hot.

This was Stewart's fourth and final trip in with logs, which was hard, quick work, since he'd trailed a half mile deep to cull proper chestnut, eight inches thick, for the side walls. Sweat streamed from his body and each naked shoulder supported a light log. Deftly he weaved between trees and circled clumps of hucklebush. Near the rear of the cabin, his ears picked up voices.

Mrs. McCaffrey, he thought, but not Mr. McCaffrey.

Stealing alongside the cabin, he spotted two talkers in the clearing and paused to listen. Mrs. McCaffrey faced a thickset man who wore a store hat and Sunday clothes.

"If there is ever any more trouble here," the man was saying, "you phone me in a hurry."

"Thank you, Mr. Simonds. The robbery didn't worry us because we carry ample insurance. However, Mr. McCaffrey insisted that I phone you and establish an official record of the theft. Have you learned anything?"

"Just that I figure the thief is a local Hill man. I passed word around the Valley, and folks will call me if the thief tries to peddle any of the loot."

"You're sure the thief is a Hill man?"

Simonds nodded.

"I like the Hill men I've met at Tamburn's store," Mrs. McCaffrey mused. "They seemed perfectly respectable."

"They fooled you, ma'am. Hill men are sly, like skunks. They are inbred and crossed with Indians and that makes 'em meaner."

"Perhaps we fail to understand them because they are so different from us. They live in such a starkly realistic environment with no modem conveniences. Walled apart from our world, they lack the education that is necessary to understand us. So they are silent and watchful in our presence." Her voice quickened. "I have the very definite impression that these people do not live in our century, because history marched past them. For them—oh, I have the right expression, Mr. Simonds! Their clock runs slow."

"Huh?"

"They live by the code of their grandfathers."

"They break the law."

"Not if you understand their outmoded code. Take that stalwart young savage who is building this cabin." Mrs. McCaffrey swiveled and spotted Stewart. He inched forward. "There you are!"

Simonds snapped: "How long you been listening there?"

Watchfulness filled Stewart's eyes.

"I'm talking to you, boy! How long did you spy?"

Stewart stood motionless.

"March here," Simonds ordered.

Mrs. McCaffrey suggested: "Please come closer."

Her words tugged Stewart to the edge of the open space.

Simonds whispered to Mrs. McCaffrey. Stewart's deer ears heard the man say: "He's an Indian. Watch me cut him down to size.

"Boy," Simonds said loudly, "I'm the law around here. What's your full name?"

Stewart thought: Talk to a pine.

"Where were you last Friday night?"

When Stewart did not answer, Simonds flared: "You'll find out I can be tough, boy! You answer my questions. Now, what's your name? How old are you? Where the hell do you hole up? Where were you last Friday night?"

The questions spilled off the knoll.

"You dumb Indian, you get one more chance to answer! Did you rob the McCaffrey house?"

Honest anger riled Stewart. Smoothly he swung the logs around. The front tips brushed the crown of Simonds' hat. That was the only warning Stewart offered. When he whipped the logs in the opposite direction, his shoulders lowered. Simonds ducked. The logs whizzed through the space where his head had been.

Simonds roared: "Watch that stuff!"

Stewart's left shoulder sagged. A log spilled off and rolled for Simonds' feet. Simonds leaped the log. When he landed, his right hand lanced inside his coat.

"Don't loose your temper," Mrs. McCaffrey warned.

"That Indian can't—"

"Simonds," she interrupted, "he meant no harm. He just returned from a tiring trip to the woods and the log slipped." Pause. "If I need you again, I'll phone."

Simonds growled, "I'll be ready," and lumbered off.

When the man's car had driven off, Mrs. McCaffrey smiled. "You weren't the least bit frightened, were you?"

Stewart grinned.

"Simonds had a gun, you were unarmed. Yet you stood your ground unafraid." Curiosity prompted her question. "If Simonds had drawn his gun, what would you have done?"

A crow flapped toward the knoll, veered off at the sight of two persons. Somewhere a woodpecker hammered on a dead log and a hawk whistled.

Effortlessly Stewart whipped the second log around. With both hands gripped to the sleek roundness, he leaned backward, then snapped his wide shoulders forward. The log hurtled through space. Belly-high, the front end sailed through the exact spot where Simonds had stood. The log crashed. The sound winged off.

Mrs. McCaffrey stared in awe.

"I ain't a thief," Stewart said quietly.

As if someone were prodding her from the rear and she could not resist the pressure, Mrs. McCaffrey flowed forward. Eyes alive, cheeks flushed, she said urgently: "You would have mashed Simonds with that—that log! Your strength was so—so wonderful!" For a long moment she studied his impassive face. "Stewart, are you listening?"

He did not answer.

She sure is a spunky little woman, he thought. She spoke and her words stopped Simonds as if he had banged into an oak. And ke-rist, she was pretty! That sweater was hoop-tight over her little breasts. Why was she atremble like an aspen in the breeze?

Young Mrs. McCaffrey flattened both palms against Stewart's naked chest. Her fingers inched upward, then blood-red fingernails dug deep into his shoulders.

"You cold brute!" she moaned.

A stallion's blood churned in his loins.

She ain't a Hill woman, he remembered. She is tiny an' can't bear the full weight of you.

"Days I've waited!" she gasped. "Are you stone?"

He wrapped an arm around her waist.

When their lips met, she was greedy. His arm tightened.

She breathed: "Not up here!"

"Hush," he said thickly.

There on the knoll, full in the hot sun, on the soft carpet of pine needles, it was an elemental, reckless thing between them. Afterward, he remembered: She bore the full weight of you. It was his only thought.

CHAPTER THREE

FULL OF YOUNG ANIMALISM, ax and sharper adze riding one shoulder, barrel chest thrust forward, Stewart kicked up road dust as his legs ate up the miles toward home.

Good day, all of it, he reflected.

Back there on the carpet of pine needles, young Mrs. McCaffrey had said: "You don't need to work today."

"Got to show something for a day's pay, ma'am."

"You showed me something!"

"I meant, something for Mr. McCaffrey to judge."

"He won't notice how much work you did."

"A man pays good wages and he knows what work is done. I got to adze the logs flat and ax notches."

"You may fix exactly one log!"

One log…

"Stewart, do you love me?"

"I ain't long on words, ma'am."

"Let me teach you what to say." She had whispered. "Will you repeat that?"

He did.

"Now, tell me something from your mind, Stewart."

"You are pretty as a doe in spring and your skin is white as dogwood blooms. You smell sweet as lilacs and they have stood all night in the lonesome rain."

"That's the perfume I wear so you'll notice me! I thought you were colder than these wintry hills, but it simply took time to thaw you out."

She sure was a talking woman.

"Stewart, did you ever love another girl?"

"Not rightly."

"Never been in love until now?"

"Didn't mean *that*."

"You were in love once?"

"Truly."

"Is this girl pretty, Stewart?"

"Yes."

"Pretty as I?"

"Well—"

"Stewart, as young as I?"

"She was some younger, ma'am."

Suddenly: "Did you take her?"

"That was once."

"You took her *once?*"

"I meant, loved her once."

"Who is this girl?"

Shut your blabmouth, he warned himself.

"Stewart, does she live on the Hill?"

"Does now."

"Is she married?"

"Truly."

"I'm glad!" She paused, then said: "You're so utterly different from us, Stewart. Taxes and modern conveniences and which way to vote never worry you. Do you know what bothered me earlier? I wondered what dress to wear at a cocktail party this coming week end!"

What's a cocktail? Stewart wondered.

"Stewart, it must be a relief to live simply."

"A man still has to feed his belly, ma'am."

"Of course, but I envy you."

"Ma'am, do Valley folks always talk like you?"

"Yes. We call it conversation. Suppose we lie here and I won't say another word."

For a whole minute she had shut up.

"Stewart, who did this girl marry?"

"A Hill man."

"What's he like?"

"Well, he is a heller on wheels for sure. He hunts more'n he works an' he roams the woods at night. He laughs a lot and likes to swig from a bottle of applejack. When he gets a bellyful of mountain dew, he sings a ballad or two."

"Do you know any ballads?"

"Not the tune."

"What are some of the words?"

"If life was a thing that money 'ud buy,
The rich 'ud live and the poor 'ud die."

"Stewart, that's pure Elizabethan!"

He knew a way to close her mouth....

"Stewart, tell me more about this ballad singer."

"Well, he's got a quicker temper than I got. He'd have slung the log at Simonds' belly and thought sense later. This man, he always carries a big chip on each shoulder, but he don't backtrack from a fight."

"Did you fight with him?"

"Why 'ud I fight with him?"

"Over the girl!"

"I don't ask for trouble."

"So he took this girl away from you! Stewart, I believe he won the girl because he was so gay and sang her ballads that brightened her drab life."

"Warn't that way a-tall, ma'am."

"No?"

"When he married this girl, I was only a sprout an' still wet behind the ears. That's the whole of it."

Stewart stopped remembering.

At the crossroads, he entered the store and dropped a nickel on the counter. "I buy a bag of sweets for John's two sons," he told old Tamburn.

Tamburn filled a bag and took the nickel. "Boy," old Tamburn said, "you just did a long day's work. What in tarnation makes you so full of ginger?"

"A bee stung me."

"Wish I was young again."

"Why?"

"Know a girl or two I'd spark."

When he was opposite the Dunn place, cooking smells eddied along the road and teased Stewart's hungry belly. He hollered at old Pete: "Car run yit?"

"She needs a thingamajig."

"What kind?"

"Don't know. I git hit an' she runs good agin."

Stewart passed on and turned into the Yeoman lane. On the roof of John's tumbled cabin, flattened tin cans patched the weathered shingles. Yellowed newspapers plugged several broken windowpanes and the door stood open on loosened hinges. Mounting the sagging porch, Stewart sang out: "John, how was your woods bed last night?"

Nobody answered.

He peered into the main room. There were a couple of broken chairs, a table covered with a clean cloth, a busted clock over the fireplace, two red geraniums blooming at the south window, and not much else, except the scrubbed look of Nelda's work.

Must be, he decided, they are all up to the house listenin' to John's brag.

In the setting sun, the Yeoman house stood solid and comfortable. In the back yard, Stewart yelled: "Hey, Tad an' Ned! I fetched that candy!"

After a moment Nelda ran out with young Tad at her heels. Next Gran sidled forth and she carried little Ned.

"You're home!" Nelda cried.

"Where is the old man and John at?" Stewart noticed the drawn, worried lines on Nelda's white face. "Hey, did Corbett catch the men and lug 'em off to Valley jail?"

"It's far worse!"

"What's up?"

"The—the dog!"

"Shep?"

"Not a half hour back," Gran whined, "Shep drug hisself home. All day I set in this poor house and felt in my bones—"

Stewart yelled: "Where's that dog?"

"By the s-stove," Nelda stammered.

Not caring if the blades smacked stone, Stewart flung the ax and adze aside. Long strides hurried him to the stove, where a huge dog sprawled. After the lean, hard winter, the dog was all massive ribs, leg muscles, and iron jaw. Burdock burrs and swamp muck dirtied the thick brown coat. Its pads were torn and bloody, its belly raked raw. Dried blood streaked the muzzle and bloody froth blubbered from the slack mouth. The dog lay exhausted, eyes lidded and breathing labored.

Stewart knelt and fingered an eyelid open. "Shep," he said gently, "you tell me."

The eye was bloodshot. When the dog did not stir, Stewart searched the matted coat and located a bullet hole near the spine.

"All day," Gran whimpered, "I had the bad feelin'. That dog is a bad sign. I tole this dumb Valley woman the men ain't comin' home, 'cept feet fust."

Stewart straightened slowly.

"What's so bad about Shep crawlin' home where he belongs?" he asked casually, while his mind groped for an explanation of the puzzle. "In a lotta ways, Shep was a dumb dog. He run too free, I always said. Some game-hungry bastard took a potshot at what he thought was a deer. That's because Shep is so big and brown. I warned the old man and John a hundred times not to let Shep run free. A Valley bastard shoots anything that moves."

"All my Yeoman men gone," Gran wailed, "an' only my baby Stewart to fend for me! Here in this house my tired feet are half-way to my bury hole!"

"That's enough of that talk," Stewart said harshly, not conscious that he talked like the old man.

"What does it mean?" Nelda asked.

"Oh, nothin' much. Guess I got to fetch the men home, is all." Crossing the room, he lifted his rifle from the pegs. "Two grown men an' they are lost in the woods. I'll carry the gun along in case I bump into Corbett." The metal chilled his stiff fingers and he tried not to show his worry. "Maybe the men need sugar pap!" He loaded the rifle and dropped spare cartridges into a jacket pocket. "Might try some target practice on the way. Might be I'll meet a buck that tries to sniff my breath!" That was the way John always talked, full of nonsense.

Turning to Nelda, he said: "You keep the victuals hot for the starved men." To Gran: "Give this bag of candy to the sons and see they don't fall into the spring." He snuggled the rifle carelessly under a crooked elbow. "I be only a half hour or so."

Right after he stepped outside, the door closed. He turned curiously. Nelda had followed him outside. She whispered fiercely: "Don't go to the woods alone!"

He waited.

"You fooled Gran, but you don't fool me! You know this is awful bad!"

"What's bad about it?"

"That bullet hole in Shep! Your father, he always talked about—a bushwhacking!"

"That was his sly joke."

"Take neighbors with you!"

"No need to fret."

"For God's sake," Nelda cried out, "won't a Yeoman ever listen to sense?"

"I ain't a boy exactly. Look, the woods is second home to me an' I know it inside out."

Without a sound, Nelda sagged against him. Stewart wrapped a free arm around her shaking shoulders and held her erect. Braced for the length of four heartbeats, he drank in the soft, shivering, clinging sweetness of her body. He thought: Nelda is a sweet armful for a man to hold, but you got business. Patting her back, he pulled free reluctantly.

Nelda moaned: "Stewart dear, if both men don't come back, what chance has one man alone?"

"Ain't no real fear."

"You've got to listen to me!" Nelda's face quivered. "Do you remember what John always said if anything happened to him? You are to take care of the sons!"

He shook his head sadly and turned away.

When he reached the backhouse, he waved to Nelda, a signal that there was no danger. Strolling past the shed and alongside the barn, he arrived in the hollow below Lonesome Ridge. When the hollow hid him from Nelda's eyes, he began to run.

In the gathering twilight with the low-hanging clouds drifting in like black, billowy pillows, he changed into a swift shadow—silent, deadly, and unafraid. In his dark hawk's eyes, the predatory gleam of a killer showed.

CHAPTER FOUR

BECAUSE HE HAD RACED OFF like a man crazed, Stewart was sorely winded as he burst into rolling land. He slowed, caught his wind, and noticed deer sign. That changed him into a Hill man, all eyes and ears and nose.

This way, he reasoned, the old man and John passed yesterday afternoon, each with a rifle and John with a bull's-eye lantern under his coat. The men planned to still-hunt, which meant cover lots of ground.

What had kept them so long?

Maybe they wounded a big buck that had knives for hoofs and razors for antlers to rip a man to shreds. Certain sure, a wounded buck would turn on a man, but could a buck kill *two* men? Not top hunters like the old man and John. They had sense to fan out when a wounded buck charged.

Because of Shep, this was worse than a wounded buck. Shep meant men. Valley spookers, maybe. It took Valley men to gun a dog.

Or maybe Warden Corbett was at the bottom of this.

Once Corbett had caught John with fresh venison out of season and the two men had bitter words. John had warned: "Next time I won't be so careless, Corbett. I'll pour the bullet into you, not the deer."

Did Corbett trail the Yeomans into the woods yesterday? Did he bushwhack them? Hardly. Corbett wasn't smart enough to outsmart two Yeomans, but it was like him to gun the dog.

The terrain roughened.

Flaunting its cotton tail patch, a spooked rabbit jounced away. That slowed Stewart. Corbett had said: "Shots last night." Caleb Hall had said: "Shots as I come up the Valley road." Valley spookers loose in these woods?

At the outermost end of Lonesome Ridge, Stewart mounted toward the wind notch. When he was halfway up the steep slope, skunk smell stung his dry nostrils, and he found the black-and-white, tom carcass. A dog had killed the skunk; must be a Valley dog to tackle a stink sprayer.

The wind notch loomed at the crest, a good place to wait for a deer to walk through at dawn or dusk. Here Stewart found nothing, and he followed a snaking deer trail down the opposite slope. Twenty minutes from home, he reached the inner Valley floor.

On the right, a spring fed a rill, and the rill seeped from its channel to sponge a broad place across the trail. Spring's first gentle footsteps, hundreds of violets flowered in the dusk, and bloodroot glowed like white stars. On the sponge, Stewart found the dotted spoor of rabbits, the tracery of mice, the child's feet of raccoon, and the old man's light steps. John's tracks were larger, heavier on the heel, and longer in stride.

This was a strange wilderness of upheaved boulders, dense stands of hardwood, tangles of brush and vines. A chipmunk, a cute handful of teeth and striped fur, whipped under a fallen log.

That standing shadow!

In one smooth, co-ordinated movement, Stewart leveled the rifle and thumbed the safety off. The tall shadow melted into the brush. There was no more sound than a shadow crossing the roof, and that proved it a buck. A doe was slower, not so silent, as if it knew less danger.

The shadows deepened.

Black as a trout's fins, clouds drifted in. Night touched the treetops and tarred the pines. The trail curled into a familiar valley that widened westward into the heart of the wilderness. Where two rills formed a brook, Stewart noted more tracks of the men and followed singing water to a pond that reflected the last light.

It was a desolate spot, a perfect deer haunt. Swamp maples burned redly in bud, bushes crowded the shore, cattails wet their feet, pickerel weed greened the shallows, and lily pads floated. Shrill peepers piped and a mud turtle rolled off a log. Amid swamp marigold there were more tracks, and Stewart trailed around the pond and down the outlet brook for a hundred yards until he lost the trace. This was the most puzzling place, because the men might head six which ways.

Stewart leaned against a wolf oak and tried to insert himself into the minds of the old man and John. Because he knew their habits well, he seemed to hear the old man's whisper.

"We shook Corbett. I favor Beaver Pond."

"I say Mason land," John argued.

"Let Masons stick to their huntin' land an' we cling to our'n, like Hill code warns. You are a wild, reckless bastard on the trail an' I don't head into bad trouble. If you'd lived as long as me, you'd not head for a likely bushwhackin' spot."

An owl hooted.

Which way?

Well, sunset and sunrise is the time to look for deer. If a man stays out late or rolls out early, he is sure to come home with fresh meat.

They should have been back for breakfast.

A deer is a critter born to hide and roam rough land with more speed and less sense than a man's smart legs. If men spook a deer, they send their dog after it to make it circle back.

They should have been home for noon.

In late April, a buck is tamer. But no buck ever exactly walked up to a man and said, "Gun me, I lived long enough." What a deer had the most of was time. Shiftless John had plenty of time, so did the patient old man. Up here, time was nothing, unless you worked at the McCaffreys', and Mrs. McCaffrey was so love-starved...

They should have been back for supper!

That black thought goaded him up the north slope. There was no trail. The steepness anchored his sense to the climb and let dread thoughts sleep in the back of his mind. Atop the crest, the night lightened.

Shrouded in darkness, the valley of Beaver Pond stretched below. A breeze hummed in to finger his sweaty face and a big brook flung up endless music.

Stewart called: "Oh, John!"

The sound winged downslope. After a spell, the echoes charged back twice, one echo from either valley.

"John!"

Time and again, Stewart filled the night with sound, but only his voice returned. So he fired the rifle and let thunder roll off. Loading carefully, he fired a second shot, then a third in signal. Nothing but his own noise came back.

"Ain't no sense to work that blackness," he muttered. "No damn sense a-tall. Go home and seek tomorrow."

For the second time he became the blind hunter.

When he plunged down toward Beaver Pond, a rock tripped him and he fell flat and lost his rifle. Cursing, he located the rifle and raced on. Creeper vines spared his feet. Briers tore his pants. A tree rose to smack him. When he strode the flat top of a rock, he stopped in the nick of time at a ledge's brink. He circled back and hurried downward. The brush thickened toward the bottom.

A branch raked an eyeball. He rubbed the smart with dirty knuckles.

Hours later, he paused far below Beaver Pond. For a long moment he eyed the mute sky and the distant shine of a billion stars. For the first time in his young life, the wilderness was an awesome, perilous thing, and the fears in his mind overflowed.

He mourned, "Ain't never to see the old man an' John alive agin," and he sobbed silently.

In the main room of the cabin, Gran slept in the old man's barrel chair and Nelda dozed in lamplight. At the sound of Stewart's light step, Nelda roused.

"You found them?" she asked in a soft, don't-wake-Gran voice.

"Where's Shep at?"

"He died."

Stewart slumped.

Nelda asked: "Are the men alive?"

"They got to be. I found their track an' lost it. The woods is a mighty place to seek."

"Did you shout?"

"Shouted an' fired three signal shots above Beaver Pond."

"The men don't answer?"

"Guess they don't hear," Stewart said stubbornly, clinging to a straw. "Where are the sons?"

"In the wall bunk."

Stewart tiptoed to the bunks and stared at two dark heads on a white pillowcase.

Nelda's raw whisper reached him. "Our men were bushwhacked!"

"Nobody durst, not with me around."

"If they were?"

"By God, I'll kill who done it!" He stood braced, body taut, hands clenched. "The Hill is a hard place. You are from the Valley and don't know our code. If the men be dead, I got to square the wrong. If I don't stand up for my kin, the dead Yeomans'll rise from their haunt holes and wing the lonesome night."

"It was good of you to seek so long." She walked to him. "You are brutal hurt and I thank you kindly."

"The men ain't dead."

"Shhh, don't wake Gran. I can't stand any more of her whining." Nelda fingered his torn coat. "You must be starved, Stewart dear. I'll cook food and set out hot coffee."

"The men ain't dead!"

Nelda nodded and forced Stewart to sit at the table. She fetched hot coffee, added milk and sugar. "See, I remember the way you like it! Don't worry. My mother always said things are never so bad as first sight makes out."

The coffee lay in his empty belly like an ember. He finished the food and relaxed. She bathed his scratched, bruised face with warm water.

"I feel better," he decided. "I will make flares of rags an' kerosene to light the way."

"You go back tonight?"

"Got to."

"Stewart, Gran said we were to stay here for a spell. Do you mind if I sleep in your bedroom?"

"The roof don't leak up here."

"I'll carry the flares."

Nelda entered the bedroom and returned with a pair of long woolen stockings. "To keep my legs warm," she explained, a secretive smile on her face. She sat on a bench and kicked off her shoes, drawing Stewart's eyes.

Crossing her legs, Nelda slipped on a stocking that had been knitted from carded wool off the Starr sheep. Against the darkness of her tanned skin, the wool glowed like snow. Inch by inch his eyes followed the length of leg disappearing within the upward pull of the stocking. When Nelda uncrossed her legs, the dress rode across her bare thighs. She smoothed the wool. Next she slid a round garter over the stocking, anchored it above her knee, then folded the top snugly to hide the garter.

"I feel warmer," she murmured.

Using the same routine, she donned the second stocking. She asked: "Ready for the woods?"

Stewart's eyes jerked up. "Huh?"

"I'll seek with you."

She is so soft, he thought. Can't let her go to the woods.

"Nelda, I changed my mind. Flares ain't much at night."

Rising, he stretched and fingered a rafter.

Nelda said: "You are so very tall."

He flattened both palms on the ceiling.

"Taller than John," Nelda added.

"I am wider through the shoulders, too."

"You are a fine man, just the one to take over this house. Gran is old and needs your great strength. So do the sons." Nelda's eyes closed. "I don't count."

I love you, he thought simply.

"Tomorrow," Nelda suggested, "take neighbors to help search the dangerous woods."

"Not yet. I don't rest till I find the old man and John." New strength surged in his body. "I'll seek everywhere an' no moss'll grow under my shiftin' feet."

"I am afraid for you." Nelda rose and walked to him. "Promise to be careful." She sagged against him. "I am—so very—tired."

She was such a scared little thing.

He wrapped an arm around her waist. The irresistible urge to kiss her dominated his thoughts. He tilted her chin.

"Valley woman," Gran whined, "where you at?"

Nelda slipped free.

"My man and John home yit?"

"Your man son is home, Gran."

"John, tell me where you been!"

"I meant *Stewart* is back."

"Oh." Gran rose and tottered forward. "Boy, do you find my men?"

"They visit a second cousin's down Tuxedo way."

"With Feeney Smith?"

"That's it."

"Feeney don't live no more at Tuxedo. Last New Year's night, he got hisself kilt in a car." Gran moaned. "All my men gone an' nobody to fend for poor me. I got nothin' but bad troubles."

"No cause to fret," Stewart said kindly. "For sure, the men'll be home tomorrow. You are tired an' need the bed." He swung Gran up, carried her into the old man's room, and stretched her on the mattress. "Get some sleep. Trouble ain't ever so bad as first sight makes it out."

He closed the door and turned to Nelda. His bedroom door had closed and he listened to Nelda's sounds in there. When the springs creaked, he sat at the table.

Suppose John is alive, eh? he wondered. Suppose John returns an' takes up where he left off, not fendin' proper for the sons, not takin' good care of Nelda, but raisin' hell an' lookin' for trouble? Why, down in that leaky cabin, John 'ud bed with Nelda and—

"Not that!" he growled, his face and hands working. "By God, John best not come home agin!"

But if John does?

I'll fix him good, Stewart thought, and he went to bed.

CHAPTER FIVE

FOR TWO DAYS Stewart combed the woods.

This day at sunset he returned and scowled at what he saw in the back yard. Unnoticed, the handful of arbutus that he had fetched for Nelda slid from his hand.

Mrs. McCaffrey sat at the wheel of the blue car. The Yeomans, three neighbors, Caleb Hall, and Corbett stood there.

Old Pete Dunn cackled: "This blue car is like mine."

"How come?" Red Scomp asked.

"Well, mine ain't got no top, neither!"

Somebody asked: "Your old car ever run?"

"That time, she had wings. I sail downhill and hit a tree ker-smack. Damme, the steam sizzled from the bust radiator and I landed on my backside with the wheel in my hand!"

Corbett announced, "Stewart's home," and everybody turned.

"Boy," Caleb drawled, "you look tuckered out."

"Warn't from squattin' on my backside all day," Stewart snapped, and nodded to Mrs. McCaffrey.

Corbett wanted to know: "You find the men?"

"That's my business."

"Have you notified the State Police?"

"It ain't their business."

"Are the men hiding from something?"

Stewart waited.

Corbett asked: "They went deer hunting?"

Red Scomp scowled. Neil Pitt and his neighbor stood like oaks. Old Pete's face warned: Mind your own business, Corbett.

Gran knew this was man's business and kept silent. When young Tad whined, Nelda shut him up with a cuff.

Corbett ignored the signs.

"I'll get to the bottom of this mystery," he promised, "I've told all Hill men not to hunt out of season. No good will come if men carry guns into the woods whenever they please. I know you've parceled out the woods for your special hunting grounds, but that don't mean you have a right to hunt any time on state land." Corbett's jaw was a rugged line. "Because you've always hunted when and how you pleased don't mean you can keep that up. I have orders. Illegal hunting has to stop."

It was a long speech, and perhaps Corbett should not have risked such words.

Nelda bundled young Tad into the house. Gran followed with little Ned. Old Pete Dunn whispered to Mrs. McCaffrey and she let the blue car roll down the grade.

"Stewart," Corbett continued, "did your men set out the other day to gun a deer illegally?"

Hill men began to ring Corbett's back.

"Stewart, do you want the State Police in here?"

Stewart scowled.

"Twice I searched the woods. I found no trace of the men. What's it mean?"

"This is Yeoman land," Stewart advised. "You got no right to come here an' jaw."

Corbett countered: "Do you want the men found?"

Nobody answered.

"Damnit, suppose the men were bushwhacked?"

"Heard enough jawin'," Stewart said, and raised his rifle. "Across the meadow, I see a knot on the top fence rail by a birch."

Stewart squared around, left hip pointed at the distant fence. Wedging the rifle butt to his shoulder, he snicked off the safety. The barrel steadied.

"Corbett, watch that knot."

Holding his breath, Stewart squeezed the trigger. The gun roared. Splinters flew from the rail. The knot disappeared.

Neil Pitt spat tobacco juice. "Stewart," he said, "called his brag an' met it."

"Damn good shot," Red Scomp said.

Caleb drawled, "If a man hinted he didn't want me on his place, I'd get the hell off."

"Keep out of this," Corbett warned Caleb.

Caleb's pig eyes turned mean.

"Don't tell me what to do, Valley man. By God, maybe this has already been atween you and John Yeoman. You said you'd git John someday. You are a mean, houndin' Valley bastard! I ask *you.* Why ain't the Yeomans home from the woods? Did you trail 'em and shoot 'em?"

"That's a lie," Corbett said thickly.

"Only askin' the truth," Caleb drawled.

Corbett noticed the threatening ring of men. He knew this was a tight spot. Sweat beaded his face.

"Stewart," Corbett said, "that was a good shot, but you aren't the only marksman."

Corbett drew his holstered .38. "I see a pine knot on the barn." Corbett thumbed the safety. "Third board from the left comer." The revolver leveled. "About eight feet high, Stewart." Corbett fired. A hole sprouted where the knot had been.

In the sudden silence, Nelda left the house carrying a milk pail. "Shame on you," she said sharply. "Grown men playing with guns and scaring the sons!" She headed for the barn.

"I may be a Valley bastard," Corbett said, and grinned, "but that was a pretty good shot."

He wheeled on the Hill men at his back. With the .38 dangling, Corbett eased forward. The circle parted to let him through. At the cabin comer, Corbett warned: "Stewart, I've always treated you fairly. Don't listen to lies about me and John. I don't gun men in the back. If you want to keep silent, that's your business. Look for State Police in the morning. They'll locate the men."

Corbett strode downhill.

Neil Pitt said: "He stood ground like a Hill man."

"He don't show no fear," Stewart agreed.

Caleb said: "If Yeomans be dead, maybe it's Corbett. He sure hated John."

Old Pete asked: "Stewart, what is new?"

"I find no more trace of the men."

"I say true," Red Scomp offered, "the men ain't near Primrose Brook, an' I looked."

"Nor to Tamarack Swamp," Neil Pitt added.

"I would search," Caleb said, "but I ain't good in the woods."

"You can say that agin," old Pete agreed.

Neil Pitt's neighbor rubbed his beard. "Sure is strange the men hunt a deer an' don't come right home. Stewart, where did they aim to hunt?"

"Can't say rightly."

"John—he is a reckless man. Heard him say to Tamburn's store he knew about a big buck to Half Moon Mountain."

"That be Mason hunting ground," Red Scomp muttered. "If Masons met John there, it's bad trouble."

"Guns speak," old Pete said.

The Masons lived across the big lake. There were the old man and three sons.

Old Pete told Stewart: "Boy, I been around longer'n you. My guess is there was a bushwhackin' party an' the old fear is loose. If 'twas Masons or other buggers, they know you will go after 'em. You keep your eyes peeled and rifle ready. This ain't the fust time men was bushwhacked."

The men nodded.

Red Scomp promised, "I will search in the morning," and he went off with old Pete.

Neil Pitt said, "We will seek to Lake Stahahe," and he and his neighbor headed toward the orchard.

Caleb bragged: "I sure told Corbett a thing or two!"

Stewart waited.

"I didn't know Corbett was such a crack shot," Caleb admitted. "Don't trust that bushwhacker. Know for a fact Corbett lugs a thirty-five rifle in his car. Say he saw Yeomans head for the woods an' he followed. Nobody is around to see what happens next. What about Corbett gunnin' Yeomans for spite?"

"It ain't the way you tell it. If 'twas, we'd be seeking Corbett, not Yeomans."

"The men to Tamburn's store figure it was Corbett or the Masons. Here's something you don't know, Stewart. Last night I was downhill again an' drinking beer at Nauright's. One of the Mason tribe sneaked in. He got a hideful of booze and bragged he knew about a big black thing had happened in the woods."

"Which Mason?" Stewart prompted.

"Not Big Ace. Not Darl, the fighter. It was Jeff, the Weasel."

"Weasel give hint what it was he knew?"

"No. I was you, I'd go after the Masons or Corbett."

Stewart decided: "First, I find the men."

"You leave for the woods at dawn?"

"Can't wait. Troopers are acomin'."

"You leave tonight?"

"Soon as it turns dark."

"I'd go," Caleb said, "but I ain't good in the woods. Guess I lived too long in the Valley. Only a Hill man or Corbett 'ud get the drop on crack hunters like the Yeomans. Still, if I owned a gun, I'd seek your kin."

Stewart stared moodily at Caleb.

The huge man wore a neat blue shirt and dark pants held up with a silver-buckled belt. His tan shoes were meant for village streets, not the rough trails. Also, he wore a new straw hat.

Caleb is right about hisself, Stewart thought. He is a porch-settin' man. The woods is for men.

"I been neighborly," Caleb continued, "and told what I know. It's Corbett or the Masons to the bottom of this."

Stewart nodded.

"I hope you git 'em," Caleb said, and headed home.

Stewart stood and thought.

The barn door closed and Nelda set the catch. Lugging a milk pail, she crossed the yard and found the arbutus Stewart had dropped.

"These for me?" Nelda asked.

"Well, I see 'em in the leaves and don't want to trample 'em."

"You're a dear, Stewart!"

Later, Nelda called from the house: "Your supper is smoking hot, Stewart dear."

In her hair she wore arbutus.

Stewart thought: I am with her and my tongue is tied, but the arbutus speaks my love.

CHAPTER SIX

A
FTER SUPPER VICTUALS, Gran sneaked into the old man's room and Nelda tidied up. She asked: "How was the supper?"

"Corn bread was best," Stewart decided.

"It only took a minute to whip sour milk and soda with ground meal like my mother taught."

"Who picked the danderlion greens?"

"I. My father says everybody needs greens in the spring."

The sons frolicked on a bearskin. Stewart asked curiously: "You always do as your father speaks?"

Nelda smiled. "That is *your* way."

"Ain't it best what my old man taught?"

Nelda paused in her work.

"I suppose," she mused, "that new ways come hard to a son on the Hill. John is like your father, only wilder. You are different. Will you fix the sons for bed, please?"

"Sure."

"John never bothered with that chore."

Stewart carried the sons outside to wet, washed their faces at the sink, and laid them side by side in the lower bunk. Then Nelda kissed each son three times.

"One from me," she hummed, "one from Daddy dear, and the last from your uncle dear!"

When Nelda had curtained the bunk, Stewart said: "I will need food to carry off tonight."

"You leave now?"

"Corbett fetches troopers in the morning. If they come, tack a rag to the barn."

"Why not let the troopers find the men?"

"Nelda, this is Yeoman business."

"If the men are dead?"

"Yes."

"That's what your father taught, Stewart?"

"That's what Gran'ther taught him, too."

While Nelda packed food, Stewart collected gear, then wrapped food and gear inside a blanket.

Again, Nelda suggested: "Let's wait for the troopers to help. My father always said—"

Stewart laughed.

"Why do you laugh?"

"You always stick by what *your* father taught, but I'm wrong to heed mine." Stewart shook his head. "Guess I don't understand a woman's mind. I'm gone, you mind your p's and q's."

Puzzled, Nelda asked: "What do you mean?"

"Caleb Hall."

"What about Caleb?"

"Lollygaggin'."

"You think I lollygag with Caleb?"

"Well," Stewart said, "he dipped your bucket full for you and rubbed agin your hip 'tother mornin'. At Mrs. McCaffrey's blue car, he stood next to you."

"Stewart, are you jealous of Caleb?"

"He needs his hide tanned!"

"Because he dipped my bucket?"

"I don't want him on my place!"

"Stewart, do you lollygag with Mrs. McCaffrey?"

He stared.

"Stewart, today she looked like she owned you."

"She don't."

"Did you tumble her?"

"No!" he growled.

"Now you're angry. Why did you give in to her?"

"Woman," Stewart sputtered, "you twist the truth!" He grabbed up rifle and blanket. "Troopers come, tack up that rag."

"I wish you wouldn't try to act like John! Just be your own true self, not like other Yeomans."

"What's wrong with Yeomans?" Stewart demanded.

"They aren't gentle and kind to me and the sons, like you are. John is a know-it-all and so is your father."

"Don't you say aught agin my kin," Stewart snapped, and hurried outside.

It wasn't right for Nelda to talk against Yeomans, not while she was wedded to John and lived in the old man's house.

Below the back yard, starlight lighted the empty meadow. From Hall land, a light shone from the kitchen window. Caleb, he thought, best stay right in the kitchen where he sets now. Facing the patch, he stared toward the orchard where the dead Yeomans rested. A black cloud loomed in the northwest.

He muttered, "Rain tonight," and took a swift step.

A rifle spoke. From the orchard, flame spurted, and a bullet whined past his ear. He plunged to the hard ground. Again flame flickered in the orchard and a second bullet hummed overhead. Stewart snapped a shot toward the orchard.

Nelda called: "Stewart?"

In the half darkness, Stewart reloaded. He peered along the rifle barrel, nostrils flaring in and out.

Carrying a lantern, Nelda ran outside. "Stewart?"

Flickering light dug into the shadows. It found him.

"Stewart, you're all right?"

He warned: "Shut up."

From a spot nearer the road, the bushwhacker fired. The bullet kicked dust a yard from Stewart.

"Git rid o' that lantern!" he ordered.

Nelda extinguished the flame. Running steps crossed to him and Nelda dropped beside Stewart.

"What is it?" she stammered.

"Bushwhacker."

"You're hurt?"

"He missed."

"Stewart, who is he?"

"Don't know, but I aim to find out." Stewart rose to his knees.

"What are you going to do?" Nelda whimpered.

"Git him."

She clung to him. "Don't go!" she pleaded.

Stewart pulled loose and ordered: "Git inside an' bolt the door." Crouching, he loped off.

Stalking was something he knew. Since childhood, the old man had taught him the art.

His heart began to thump with excitement. His eyes gleamed. Planning to attack the bushwhacker from the rear, he circled far to the left. When the lowering black cloud frowned on his back, he turned downhill. Underfoot, a dead stick snapped. He waited and crouched. When nothing stirred, he moved ahead.

Gradually, tree trunks and budding branches took shape. Stewart stepped behind one trunk and searched the thick cover. Headstones reflected the starlight. The big, whitest one was for Brother George, he remembered. Quietly he slipped from tree to tree, drawing nearer to the thick brush and trees that lined the sunken road to Lake Kanawaukee.

There were two ways for the bushwhacker to escape: to this road or past the Yeoman house. At the edge of the bushy screen, he peered to the right. Then, stepping like a velvet-footed buck, he eased through the bushes and reached the dusty ditch. Carefully he searched the ground.

There!

Thirty yards to the right, a darker shadow leaned against a tree on this side of the road. Stewart crossed to the opposite side. The shadow stood immobile. Starlight glinted off a rifle barrel.

Got you, Stewart thought grimly.

When he was twenty feet from the unsuspecting quarry, the man leaned forward to peer into the orchard. Disdaining danger, Stewart closed in and rammed his rifle muzzle into the skulker's back.

"Don't move, bushwhacker," Stewart warned.

Red Scomp stood still.

"By God, you fired at me."

"Stewart, not me!"

"Three shots you fired an' missed."

"No! I hear shots an' come runnin'!"

"Why?"

"Nobody shoots on the Hill at night."

Stewart ordered: "Drop that rifle."

Red obeyed.

"Step off," Stewart ordered.

Red walked off. "I only come to help!"

"Talkin' don't git you outa this."

Stewart examined Red's rifle. The barrel was cold. He sniffed at the muzzle. Then he knew that Red spoke the truth. No odor of freshly burned powder stung his nostrils.

"I am sorry for what I suspicioned," Stewart apologized. "You see a bushwhacker sneak down this road?"

"No. I heard that first shot an' got my rifle. I saw the road when he fired a third time. Stewart, he didn't pass down."

"Then he headed to Kanawaukee."

"What do you make of this?"

"I fear for the men, Red."

"The old man and John are dead?"

"Ain't no other reason I know for a bushwhacker to fire at me. I'll head for the woods tonight. I'll thank you kindly to keep an eye on my house till I come home."

"Sure. You need more help?"

"Figure to do the job myself."

"Stewart, old Pete spoke a heap of sense today. Keep your eyes keen an' rifle ready."

"Right."

Red grumbled: "I thought we was rid of bushwhackers."

Stewart stole across the field below the orchard and stepped into the back yard. Nelda waited by the open door. Before she could speak, running feet sounded from the meadow and Caleb Hall burst into the back yard.

Caleb panted: "What the hell's goin' on?"

"A bushwhacker," Nelda explained.

Caleb wore only pants and he carried a club.

"I was dozin' in the kitchen," he growled, "an' heard shots. A bushwhacker, you say?"

"In the orchard," Nelda answered.

"Stewart, he got clean away?"

"This time he did," Stewart admitted.

Caleb swore. "Was it Corbett or a stinkin' Mason skunk?"

"Can't rightly say."

"Got to be Corbett or a Mason." Caleb peered at Stewart's starlit face. "Thought you were headin' for the woods after dark."

"Was, only this bugger fired."

"Stewart," Nelda asked, "what does this mean?"

"I fear for our men."

"They're dead?"

"Ain't no other reason for a bushwhacker to be about."

"By God," Caleb growled, "I don't like this. I came back on the Hill to seek peace an' quiet an' now we got a bushwhacker. Say, you got a spare gun?"

Stewart asked: "What for?"

"I ain't got a gun. I ain't got much sense in the woods, neither, but I can guard this house."

"Nelda'll bolt door an' windows."

As Stewart walked to the spot where he had left the blanket, Nelda called out: "Please take care of yourself!"

"Aim to."

Caleb said: "Good huntin', Stewart."

As Stewart passed from the back yard and melted into the darkness, he muttered, "Rain tonight," and went to meet the black clouds that rolled in.

CHAPTER SEVEN

FOR HOURS, the rain thrummed steadily.

Deep in the wilderness, Stewart had felled a squat balsam and had left the trunk clinging to a four-foot stump. Axing out the inner branches, he had double-thatched the top and had fashioned a sweet green tent over a thick balsam bed and had passed the night there, snug as a bug.

At crack of dawn, he awakened to a clearing sky.

From pond and swamp and swollen brook, peepers piped monotonous music. A fire-tailed warbler serenaded its drab mate. A cock partridge drummed by a fallen log.

Stewart crawled outside and stood stiff and cold. On the wet ashes of last night's warming fire he kindled a new flame, boiled coffee, and ate from the food that Nelda had packed.

He searched for two days.

Spring had awakened the land. Redbrush jumped into flower and dogwood snowed the hills. Locust trees stood like clouds of yellow mist and hardwoods leaved. Swallows swooped and caught lacewings on gummy beaks. Three white butterflies danced a ballet over Dutchmen's breeches that flowered like bits of dropped cotton. Anemones quivered on wiry stems, trout lilies and lady's-slippers bloomed riotously.

At midafternoon Stewart hurried along an old trail and stepped suddenly to the brim of Call Mountain, where he had stood a hundred times, and on pleasanter days had shouted his name. Below stretched the strange face of this inner wilderness.

Outside the Rampart, a smoke plume trailed south, and that was an Erie train poking its way toward Suffern Gap. Faint on the last horizon, the tiny towers of New York town stood, only an hour's ride in Mrs. McCaffrey's blue car.

Each May up here, Stewart thought, is a better one because you add all the other Mays into this new one.

His mind chewed on the puzzle.

He had combed every acre of Yeoman hunting grounds, and then some more. Nowhere had there been more trace of the old man and John. If he had been that black crow, he might fly up every brook, along each lonely deer walk, and across every rock spine, and from the sky spy out everything in a hurry. Up there, things were good. Sin was on the earth. Sin was where the old man and John hid. Sin was the dead Yeoman dog.

Slipping over the rim of Call Mountain, he worked downhill. Sense told him there was one spot left to seek.

Chickadees flew in and tailed along. At the valley floor he checked the way before entering a main trail. Waterfall music grew louder. Below a bright fall of water, a trout surfaced and gobbled a swimming bug. At Half Moon Mountain, where the trail forked into Yell Hollow, Stewart hopped the brook and whispered down to a wide, soft place of black dirt across the trail. Finding man's trace, he squatted to sort out the story of the tracks.

Left here before the heavy rain, the tracks were at least three or four days old. Three men had come uptrail running hard; three men had walked downhill fast. The largest prints belonged to Big Ace Mason; the lightest were those of Darl, the fighting Mason; the narrowest belonged to the Weasel.

Caleb Hall had said: "I heard the Weasel brag about some big black thing that happened in the woods."

Uphill at the fork, Stewart headed for Yell Hollow, which was the heart of Mason hunting grounds. When the brook tempted his dry throat, he sprawled on his belly. At the side of a pool, fresh raccoon tracks and a crawfish shell told that the 'coon had caught the crawfish and washed the meat in running water, because that was a 'coon's way with fresh food.

Stewart gulped sweet mountain water and sneaked inward along the trail that wandered through beech woods and lazed under spaced whitewood trees that stood straight as rulers stuck on end. The trail mounted a rise and crawled down to a wide curve that curled away from a hollow where the brook sparkled in the sun. Skunk smell drifted in strong.

By the inward curve! Stewart lunged forward.

Squarely in the middle of the trail, a dead buck with a tremendous rack lay on its flank. When the buck had fallen, one set of antlers had become embedded in the ground, and that had erected the opposite set over the trail. The buck had been gunned and gutted, but not here. Dried blood blackened the white underbelly and the brown flanks. Fat flies buzzed over the carcass. More flies crawled in and out of the rotted gut. Poisoning the clean air, making a horror of the trail, was the rank smell of death.

Three yards ahead of the buck's antlers lay the old man. Behind the buck, John sprawled.

"Bushwhacked!" Stewart cried hoarsely.

When the old man had been gunned, he had fallen forward on his face, leaving his legs fanned out, his arms outflung. Beyond the uncovered thatch of white hair on his head lay his worn cap. The fingers of his right hand still gripped his rifle. A second rifle—this was John's—rested inches from his left hand, which was palm upward toward the sky. The rain had speckled both barrels with rust.

John lay on his belly, too.

In falling, he had pitched forward so that one arm had been pinned fast under his stocky body. The fingers of his left hand were closed in a tight fist. Bullet holes pitted each Yeoman's face and clothes. Dark blood had flowed and crusted each wound. In death they waited with black, gaunt, bewhiskered faces, and wild animals had chewed...

Unnoticed, the rifle slipped from Stewart's lax fingers. He stood motionless, unable to believe the immensity of the tragedy. Stiffly, as if the sections of his powerful body worked on rusted hinges, Stewart settled to his knees. Taking off his cap, he bowed his head. When he began to speak in a monotone, the words were those of an ancient ritual, the only prayer he knew.

> "Praise God, I lay me down to sleep
> An' pray the Lord my soul to keep.
> If I should die afore I wake,
> I pray the Lord my soul to take. Amen."

It was the end of the long, tedious trail that he had followed for days. Even as he had anticipated many times, a new, more heart-breaking trail had started up on this bright May day.

CHAPTER EIGHT

FOR GENERATIONS within the challenging Ramapo wilderness, a man's fight to live had been a touch-and-go proposition. During the protracted subzero winters, when deep snow had imprisoned the land, the only factor that had stood between life and death was a man's sure grip on a rifle pointed at a deer. Venison was mountain beef; beef guaranteed survival. Too often there had been perilous climaxes when deer and even smaller game were scarce and a Hill man had hungry bellies to feed at home. Meeting at the choicest hunting spots, Hill men had battled with fists, clubs, and guns over a scrawny carcass. Men had been beaten into insensibility; men had been wounded; and two men had been brutally bushwhacked in the internecine squabbles. Finally Stewart's grandfather had taken the bit in his teeth and summoned the important families to a meeting.

"We ain't one bit smart," that George Yeoman had argued, "to add man trouble to the troubles we got to face each day. I am sick an' tired o' fussin' about a bushwhackin' when all I aim to do is live peaceful. I say the smart thing is to parcel out the huntin' ground an' let each man stick to his own place. We got to use more sense in huntin', too, and not kill fawns like some game-hungry bastards is adoin'. Hellamighty, don't gun a doe in winter 'cept it's a matter of keepin' the wolf from the door. If we do this, by Lord Harry, we live peaceful an' life ain't a question of which man is quicker with a gun an' that gun aimed at a neighbor. Am I talkin' through my Yeoman hat or do I add up to sense?"

The speech had convinced the Hill men.

Leaving open certain lands where any man with strong legs might hunt freely, the families had allotted each other special territory where only they were to hunt.

Gun your own land, the code cautioned, and live longer.

Because the Hill men had realized that the code was wise and because they had respected the code, the bitter feuding had ended abruptly. Even the deer herd had increased.

Today there was plenty of whitetail for every man, and some left over for the Valley hunters. The only present worry that a Hill man had if he craved fresh venison out of season was the need to stay clear of Corbett, the warden.

Understanding and respecting this important local history, Stewart had first searched only on Yeoman hunting ground. Later, he had sought in the lands where any Hill man was free to hunt. Lastly, his failure to find the missing men had forced him to try Mason land, which lay next to the Yeomans'.

Now, as he stood by the dead men, he realized that the smoldering dread of a bushwhacking had burst into flame again.

Murder set off more murder.

A bushwhacker fired on you from the orchard.

While Stewart knew that the Yeomans had been wrong to hunt and kill this big buck on Mason land, he knew, also, that it had been John's wild, thoughtless planning. Yet a brutal bushwhacking did not seem to be the proper penalty.

You pin this to the Mason tribe what done it, he told himself, and set to work to unravel the puzzle.

A minute inspection of the bodies uncovered six bullet holes in the old man and ten holes in John. In addition to the rifle bullet that had dropped the buck, there were three smaller holes in the carcass. Add the bullet that had killed poor Shep and that was twenty bullets, a powerful lot of shooting.

How had the Masons bushwhacked?

It had to be, because of the size of the holes, one Mason with a pump-action shotgun firing Double-O-Buck shells. Could be the Mason brothers together planned and carried out the bushwhacking. The sneakin' sons-abitches, he thought bitterly, they sure poured it into the old man and John because of one buck! Back of the rimrock that divided Hill from Valley, dead men didn't ponder questions, and they didn't rise up to speak answers, either!

Strange...

Why didn't Shep, a smart dog on the trail, nose out the bush-whackers and give warning with a bark?

Stepping off the trail on the hollow side, Stewart studied the position of the bodies. From this vantage point, he realized that every bullet wound was in their left sides. Facing the hollow, which dropped about seven feet, he peered at the terrain.

Shep didn't bark?

If that be true, he reasoned, the bushwhackers was out of nose range or the wind blew outa Yell Hollow.

His keen eyes drew an imaginary line of fire across the hollow. He centered attention on a likely place of ambush, a stand of squat balsam on the opposite slope, about forty yards distant. Jumping the bank, he stalked to the brook, but the litter of dead leaves and wild flowers yielded no clues or tracks. Before the balsam, he checked the slope. Here the leaves seemed undisturbed.

Behind the balsam, he found several places where the dead leaves were hard-packed, as though more than one man had nested here. How did Masons get the drop on the old man and John from here? Well, they knew beforehand the Yeomans meant to hunt Yell Hollow or they were lucky enough to see the Yeomans sneak through. Which way was it? He found the answer immediately.

At the height of a man's eyes, and that man kneeling, broken twigs in the balsam screen made a good spying place. Peering along that opening, he saw the trail clearly. Thus he decided that the Masons must have known the Yeomans meant to hunt here and had had plenty of time to set the ambush.

Next he knelt and carefully sifted the dead leaves. He found three ejected shells, each Double-O-Buck labeled "Remington Express." That proved the killer used a pump-action shotgun.

Stewart knew that every Double-O-Buck shell carried a charge of powder sufficient to propel nine .30-caliber pellets a distance of a hundred yards at killing force. Firing with an open choke pattern, the killer obtained a wide spread on the target. From forty yards, the killer fired first at John, who stopped most of the pellets; used a second shot for the old man and Shep.

The "pump" was simply a sliding cylinder under the barrel. A spring snapped and held the shells in a single line within this cylinder. When the cylinder was loaded with a legal charge of three shells, the killer pushed the pump forward to cock the gun, fired by trigger pull, then jerked the pump backward to eject the used shell. A pump operated just as rapidly as the killer was able to work the cylinder.

After that first shot, Stewart reasoned further, it took a little time to eject the spent shell, recharge the gun, and aim at the target. That delay gave Shep a chance to bolt part way out of range and stop only one bullet. With the men and Shep down, the killer got the hell out of here.

Which Mason had fired?

Well, Big Ace was the blabmouth.

Darl was the fighter, afraid of no man.

The Weasel was the top hunter.

Stewart's eyes hardened.

There was one last, important clue.

Buried under loose leaves, he found a footprint on rich, black dirt. It was a man's big print and the sole was not important. On the inner run of the heel, and at the back, was the print of a steel plate shaped like a half-moon and fastened with two nails.

Whose heelprint?

Not the Weasel's. Weight gouged out that print. Not big enough for Darl, the fighter. The print had to be that of Big Ace, who weighed over two hundred pounds.

Stewart erased the print. He pocketed one shell.

This was Yeoman business, nobody else's.

Back at the trail, Stewart did everything that a Hill man was expected to do for his kin. First, he hefted the stinking buck's carcass to his shoulders, and, carrying his rifle along, he lugged the carcass a hundred yards into the woods, where he hid the evidence under dead leaves and logs. Corbett wasn't going to have the satisfaction of knowing that the Yeomans had killed a buck illegally.

Back at the ambush point, he remembered that Gran had said: "John, he toted a bull's-eye lantern along to jack-light, in case they don't get mountain beef at sundown." Stewart searched, but failed to find the lantern.

Masons stole it, he decided.

Carefully he filled the antler holes with dirt, tamped the dirt smooth to erase the holes, and spread more loose leaves over the trail. Finally he lugged John close to the old man and held his breath to keep the death stench from his nostrils. Spreading the blanket over both bodies, he anchored the edges with heavy stones so that no more wild animals might chew freely on the Yeomans. There was no sense to tote their guns home, either. With the buck hidden, there was no single proof of a game law broken, and the men had a right to guns.

The sun had dipped behind a ridge. Long shadows crawled through the woods. Some of the heat left the lonely hollow. A thrush rang its bell.

You don't sit on your backside, Stewart vowed, nor do you rest in your bed till you settle for this hellish thing the Masons done. You will ferret in their dirty nest and you will find the lantern they stole. You find their shells to mate the one in your pocket. You find that shoe with that half-moon plate and the two nail holes. You do that or any part of it and you prove the Masons bushwhacked. At the end of this new trail there are three skunks to kill. No, you best make it four *skunks*. Don't leave Old Man Mason out of this. It was his worse sin to breed such sneakin' skunks. There ain't never been a good Mason, 'cept Elly, the pretty young sister. Elly can live, but nobody'll ever bear the Mason name on this hill again.

Choosing not to follow the dangerous trails, Stewart set off through the woods.

In the middle of twilight on the Hill, inside the dim Yeoman house, Gran squatted within the depths of the old man's barrel chair and cradled little Ned. Nelda stood near the hot cookstove, but she did not work with the supper. His face bright as a young raccoon's, Tad peeked around Nelda's short skirts.

Just over the sill, Stewart halted. On the walk home he had decided there was no point in beating around the bush and he blurted the truth.

"It is bad news I fetch to all the Yeomans here. The old man an' John lay dead on the trail into Yell Hollow near Half Moon Mountain and that is land the Mason tribe claims to hunt. I find sixteen bullets in their poor, tom bodies and it is a hellish thing what has happened here an' I—"

Knowing that more was wrong than the stark facts off his tongue, Stewart blundered to a stop.

The horror tale turned Nelda into a statue. The blood drained from her cheeks. She stood with mouth agape, fingers twitching. By far, Gran was the smarter of the two women, and she didn't let the truth befuddle her Hill training. While she listened to Stewart, she also peered past him, and it was Gran's stare that had warned Stewart.

He turned.

Toward the wall bunk stood a tall, strange young man dressed in the natty uniform of a York State trooper. In one hand he held a peaked hat. The thumb of his opposite hand was hooked inside a cartridge belt.

Stewart demanded: "Who be you?"

"Sergeant Donovan, sir."

Donovan stepped forward.

"Game Warden Corbett phoned the barracks that your father and brother were missing and I was detailed to the Hill. I just returned from the woods." Shock lengthened his face. "I'm sorry to hear the bad news."

Stewart scowled.

"Boy," Gran whined, "I don't tell this stranger one true fact. I don't say the same for this Valley woman an' her blabmouth. Twicet I told her to shut up, but she don't heed."

Stewart waited.

Donovan asked quietly: "Your father and brother were murdered?"

Watchfulness filled Stewart's face.

"It *is* murder?"

Wood snapped in the cookstove.

"Let's be reasonable," Donovan persisted. "Ramapo people like to keep their troubles at home, but this sounds like murder.

I'm not snooping, but asking questions." Donovan produced a notebook and pencil. "First, we'll get the facts straight, Stewart. What time did you find the bodies?"

Stewart stood silent.

"Tell all you know," Nelda urged.

Gran snapped: "Keep your blabmouth outa man's business!"

When Stewart did not offer to speak, Donovan said patiently: "You found the bodies on a trail into Yell Hollow, which is near Half Moon Mountain. That's Mason land, you said. Now, what's the shortest way there?"

Stewart thought, Don't trust a Valley man, and that was the old man's teaching.

"I'll explain the law to you," Donovan continued. "Whenever a crime has been committed, it's the duty of every citizen to aid the police. If you withhold evidence, Stewart, that's a misdemeanor. A misdemeanor is a crime. If you don't tell me what you know, you can be fined or imprisoned or both. Clear?"

"I ain't done the wrong," Stewart said stubbornly.

"If you don't tell me what you know, you've done wrong." Donovan searched Stewart's implacable face. "What about it?"

Rooted to silence by the stern Hill code, Stewart thought: It's your job, not his. 'Sides, Donovan can't find his own feet and he is in the woods.

"I have rights in this," Nelda said quietly. "Stewart, will you please speak out?"

"What I got to say," Stewart answered, "is for any man to hear. I searched long an' stumbled across the old man an' John an' they was dead. Ain't nothin' in what I done, but another man can do the same an' he's willin'."

"We'll talk outside," Donovan decided, and both men walked into the back yard.

Inside the house, Gran moaned: "I felt hit in my bones that the men is to come home feet fust on a board. Tole the men not to go to the woods. Tole 'em I had the bad feelin' in my bones. A man don't never listen to a woman what talks sense."

Outside, Donovan asked: "Do you want the murders solved?"

"Certain sure," Stewart agreed.

"Will you help me?"

"Ain't so sure I can help."

"How do we reach the bodies?"

Waving at Lonesome Ridge, Stewart said: "Beyond that."

"Will you take me there?"

"Can't find the way at night."

"Will you try?"

"The way is long."

"Two men are dead—murdered!" Donovan snapped, losing patience. "Bushwhacked, you said in the house! I won't stand and talk because you've been taught a code of silence!"

From the doorway, Nelda spoke.

"The best way to Yell Hollow is down the Sloatsburg road to the outlet brook from the lake, then past—"

"Shut your blabmouth!" Gran hollered.

"Go right past the Mason house," Nelda continued, "to the main trail alongside the lake. That takes you to Yell Hollow."

"Thank you, Mrs. Yeoman," Donovan said.

Gran hollered: "You Valley woman!"

"I've a car down the lane," Donovan said. "We'll go there first." It was an order.

At the police car, Donovan talked into a short-wave set.

"Lieutenant, Donovan calling in from the Ramapo Hill. Donovan calling in, sir. Do you hear me? Over."

A man answered.

Donovan said: "There's been a big break in the Yeoman case, sir. At six-ten, Stewart Yeoman—he's the younger brother—returned from the woods. He found his father and brother dead with sixteen bullets in their bodies. They were bushwhacked at Yell Hollow, which is near Half Moon Mountain. Over."

Donovan listened, then: "Right, Lieutenant. Stewart is taking me to the scene of ambush. Will you send more men to the Mason house? They live below the dam at the head of the Sloatsburg road. Anything else, sir?"

Donovan listened.

"Very good, sir. Signing off."

Donovan replaced the mike.

"Stewart, we'll drive to the Mason place."

It was his father's constant teaching, steeped in the elemental tradition of Hill taciturnity, that had stayed Stewart's tongue. Yet he did not wish to involve himself in trouble with Donovan.

"I sure want to help," Stewart said. "It's 'most dark, but I can find Yell Hollow."

"Do we start out by car?"

"Quickest way is with the feet."

They walked the lane and passed the Yeoman cabin. In the lowering twilight, the rich Yeoman meadow was a cup of greenness. A bluebird winged over the spring hole and that was a sure sign that summer was near. Smoke curled from the crooked chimney of the Hall cabin and a light shone from the kitchen window.

Donovan said confidently: "I'll solve this in a hurry."

"How soon is a hurry?"

"We work fast. Two or three days."

They entered the woods, Stewart in the lead.

Give me a day or two, he thought, an' there won't be no Masons left for Donovan to catch.

His stride lengthened.

CHAPTER NINE

U NDER THE GNARLED APPLE TREES where past generations of Yeomans rested, mourners stood humbly.

Among the mossed headstones, one stood out prominently because of the date of death, 1796. The faint name was that of George Yeoman, the Hill's first settler, who had come there before the Revolutionary War.

This George had taken his new bride, a span of oxen, musket and ammunition, tools and seed, but not much else, and, journeying from Hackensack in north Jersey, had reached the Suffern Gap by Indian trails, then had pushed on to where a brook from inside the Rampart entered the Ramapo River. Through virgin timber that few men had traversed, including the river Indians, he had hacked a way up Stony Brook and reached the inner wilderness.

George had settled near the present Yeoman house. Felling timber that first summer, George had built cabin and barn, and settled down to till the soil, fight the Indians occasionally, and constantly battle the animal predators—bear, cougar, and wolf. Raising crops of oats, rye, com, and vegetables that first summer, he had survived the following rigorous winter. Land was cheap, only a few pennies an acre. When he finally got around to it, George Yeoman had filed a land claim.

Often Stewart had listened to the old man narrate the accumulated legends that had been passed down by previous generations of Yeomans. Once river Indians had captured several women and girls, and had tied them to trees by the hair as a sinister warning to vacate the pioneer settlement. During the years three men and several boys had been scalped, yet the pioneers had persisted.

Another time, while the men had been out hunting, a pack of starved wolves had descended on the settlement and had slaughtered some of the livestock. Until 1806, the state had paid a bounty on these vicious predators. During and after the Revolution, outlaws and deserters from the Continental Army had sought refuge behind the isolated Rampart.

Very early the pioneers had learned never to ask questions of strangers who passed through or tarried to build a home. Through the perilous years, this attitude of taciturnity and suspicion of every outsider from the Valley had hardened into a fixed habit. Don't talk and live longer, the Hill code warned. Thus the taciturnity of the Hill men was a fundamental part of their belief, even today.

On this late afternoon in May, the hot sun hurried the apple trees into blossom and fetched hundreds of wild honeybees to forage above the gravestones. On every side hill, along the stark run of Lonesome Ridge, and fringing every edge of woods, dogwood rioted and powerful fragrance saturated the still air.

Near the open double grave, Stewart waited. He had built the bury boxes of new pine boards to hold the old man and John. He had dug that hole with a spade. He had helped lower the boxes into their bury hole. That was fit and proper for a son to do.

Around him thronged the gathered Hill folk, the men awkward and humble in Sunday clothes, the women silent and motionless in black. Not understanding this strange ceremony, young Tad and little Ned clung to a neighbor woman's skirt, and from time to time spoke in a childish treble. Gran leaned on Stewart's arm, Nelda a pace beyond Gran.

Not once does Nelda cry, Stewart thought. Why is a new widow dry-eyed?

A half-dozen Starrs were up from Sloatsburg to mourn. Neil Pitt was here with his dark wife and pack of young'uns; Red Scomp and his family; and Caleb Hall, old Pete Dunn, and Tamburn, who had closed the store for the day. There were many more Hill families, but not a single Mason man. Down by the house stood Mrs. McCaffrey's blue car, and she watched from a nearby apple tree. Off to one side, their heads together in quiet talk, were Sergeant Donovan and Warden Corbett, like outsiders.

The youthful, earnest preacher lifted his eyes from the Bible, which he had been reading. From down Haverstraw way, he was the man who preached in the tiny church every other Sunday, baptized the newly born, married the young in heart, and visited at the cabins occasionally.

Stewart cocked an ear.

In a resonant voice the preacher mingled his words with the songs of warblers.

"My good people," the preacher said, "you have just heard the words of the Gospel. I know that you understand the message. I pray that you will heed the words. On this day of sadness, I must repeat the truths that have been sounded during the years. 'Vengeance is mine,' saith the Lord, 'and I will avenge.' That teaching must guide our ways as we shape our lives to that of the Lord. Each day, as we perform our humble tasks ..."

Preacher is wrong, Stewart thought. The old man taught vengeance is our'n.

"We bow our heads together," the preacher intoned. "My good people, let us join in one last prayer for those who are no longer here to comfort us."

They bowed their heads.

"Our Father, Who art in Heaven—"

Stewart stood silent.

"And forgive us our trespasses as we forgive those who trespass against us."

Stewart shivered.

Forgive a sinning Mason? Never!

"For Thine is the kingdom, and the power, and the glory, for ever and ever. Amen."

One chore remained.

Stewart joined the preacher, who shoveled the first dirt into the grave. As the clods thudded hollowly on the bury boxes, Gran wailed piteously, but that was the only sound. Stewart took the shovel and set his shoulders to finish the task. Red Scomp and another neighbor helped.

When the fresh dirt lay mounded high, the folks formed a line and filed past. Tenderly they laid sprays of dogwood and bunches of wild flowers on the mound until the dirt had disappeared. Each person nodded solemnly to Stewart and their faces told how their hearts felt. Each person walked to Gran and Nelda, nodded, but spoke no word. Slowly they wandered down the slope and grouped by the house. When everyone had passed, Nelda steadied Gran and helped her downhill.

Mrs. McCaffrey spoke to Stewart.

"If there's anything I can do, send word. Better yet, come yourself."

She walked off.

It was over.

One task remained for Stewart—vengeance.

There in the deserted orchard, after the folks had left the Yeoman house, Sergeant Donovan and Corbett found Stewart.

"Man to man, I want to say this," Corbett said. "I never had anything personal against your father and John. This is a sad day for all of us."

Stewart waited.

"Do you feel like listening?" Donovan asked.

Stewart nodded.

"This isn't easy," Donovan began. "The State Police are investigating. We've questioned every Hill man, some of them several times. We found out some facts. One thing I must hear from you. When you were first at the ambush scene, did you remove any evidence?"

There were wormholes in the patch today, Stewart thought. 'Tis past time to spade.

Donovan said patiently: "If you won't answer a simple question, I'll tell you what we've discovered. We took six thirty-caliber bullets from your father, eleven from John. In nearby trees we located four more bullets. Another one killed Shep, the dog. That's twenty-two bullets, Stewart, more than you saw. Behind a screen of balsam across the hollow from the ambush, we located two empty Double-O-Buck shells, labeled 'Remington Express.' I figure the killer fired three shots. Does that make sense?"

Stewart nodded.

"Corbett scouted the woods around Yell Hollow and nosed out the rotted carcass of a buck. There were three more bullets in that whitetail, plus a bullet that had been fired from a thirty-five rifle. In the laboratory, our men proved the bullets were Double-O-Buck. I believe John carried that dead buck on his shoulders as he and your father walked into the ambush. By the way, what happened to the third empty shell?"

"Search me," Stewart drawled.

"It's in your pocket?"

"No."

"Another thing." Donovan's voice began to harden. "In the laboratory, our men checked the boring in the rifles your kin carried. Using the thirty-five bullet that had killed the buck, they proved that a bullet from your father's rifle dropped the buck. Do you know what a comparison microscope is, Stewart?"

"No."

"I won't explain it in detail, but it's the way we have to prove what I told you. Our men fired shots from your father's and John's rifles. They photographed the bullets for markings. That's why we know your father killed the buck."

Stewart thought hard.

"You see my old man kill that buck?" he asked.

"Of course not."

"'Less you see a man fire a gun and see the buck drop you don't know what man killed it."

"I won't argue with you, but we're right. Now—your father and brother entered lands that the Masons claim as theirs to hunt. You know that. Did the Masons bushwhack them because your father and brother broke the Hill code?"

"Can't rightly say."

"Why not?"

"I warn't there to see."

Donovan swore.

"Do you *believe* the Masons bushwhacked them?"

"I don't see 'em do that," Stewart persisted.

"Told you Stewart won't co-operate," Corbett snapped. "He's covering up something."

Donovan nodded and returned to a previous question. "Stewart, did you keep that third shell?"

"Maybe you don't find it."

Donovan lost his temper.

"Goddamnit, I know we didn't find it! We went over every inch of ground behind that balsam screen! We screened dozens of yards of dirt and leaves and we didn't find it! Did you take it?"

Stewart drawled: "You know how a pump gun works?"

"Yes!"

"And three shots was fired?"

"Yes!"

"Maybe the bushwhacker don't eject the third shell."

Donovan glared.

"That's possible," Corbett agreed. "With the Yeomans dead and the cylinder empty, the killer didn't bother to eject the third shell."

Donovan snapped: "Did you move John's body?"

"Sure," Stewart admitted.

"Why?"

"That was the human thing to do. Wild things had chewed off 'em long enough."

"That's the only reason?"

"Well, I only had one blanket to cover 'em." Humor burgeoned in Stewart's eyes. "You'll write that in your little book?"

"Never mind what I write. Now, where the buck's antlers had spiked the trail, you filled the holes with dirt. I don't give a damn about the buck your father killed. What matters is that you tramped the ground and destroyed tracks. Uh—do you know what a *moulage* is?"

Stewart shook his head.

"A *moulage* is a plaster cast the police make of any footprints. When we come across a suspect, we check his footprints against this *moulage.* If we can place any man's footprints on the trail where your men were killed, we have our killer. That clear?"

"You're sayin' it."

"The only prints we found on the trail were yours." Donovan stared hard, as if he meant to see into Stewart's mind. "Did you find any strange prints?"

"None on the trail 'cept Yeomans'."

Something that Donovan had said puzzled Stewart.

"All the time you talk," Stewart blurted, "you keep talkin' about *one* killer."

"That's right. It takes one man to work a pump-action shotgun. I'll search every Hill cabin for that shotgun, too. Did you handle those two empty shells?"

"Picked 'em up, is all."

"You certainly closed every trail to that killer!" Donovan exploded. "Did you do all those things on purpose?"

"I warn't in my right mind."

"From here on, you leave the murders to me! I can do the job better than you!"

"So you been tellin' me," Stewart drawled. "Did you catch the bushwhacker yet?"

Donovan swore.

"Stewart," Corbett asked, "what about a bull's-eye lantern?"

"Say that again."

"Did John carry one with him?"

"I don't see him."

"You needn't act dumb with me. John owns a lantern?"

"All Hill men has a lantern or two."

Down below, Nelda headed for the barn, milk pail swinging.

"If there is trouble with the cow, a lantern shows a man to the dark barn. It fetches his feet to the woodpile better. A woman has to fetch water for bedtime, a lantern lights the path to the spring hole. Up here, a lantern is a tool."

Corbett turned to Donovan.

"Now do you understand what I'm up against with Hill men?"

Donovan said: "We get nothing but lies."

"I ain't a lie-teller," Stewart said.

Corbett asked: "Where's John's lantern?"

"It warn't with him."

"I'll give you a final warning," Donovan said. "Don't butt into police business again. Don't try to find the bushwhacker. Don't plan to take the law into your own hands. I've been damned patient with you and I don't want any more runarounds."

"Ain't a lie-teller," Stewart said.

"The next time I come here to ask questions, you give the answers like—" Donovan searched for a proper expression. "Give me everything like a cow gives milk."

Stewart grinned.

"A cow don't give milk," he corrected.

"No?"

"Hell, no. You got to *pull* the milk out. You'll write that fact in your little book?"

Donovan stomped off.

Corbett smiled. "You fellows don't give a damn for nobody, I guess. About that buck your father killed on Mason land. Let's have no more of that."

"We got a right to kill a buck any time."

"That's not what the state law says."

"On the Hill," Stewart countered thoughtfully, "we ain't perticular about Valley law."

Corbett said, "If the Yeomans had respected the state law, they wouldn't lie buried," and he followed Donovan.

They got pig's wind from you, Stewart thought proudly.

He went back over the deepening puzzle. One bushwhacker? That was a Valley lie.

That Donovan was full of lies. How could he tell the old man gunned that buck when he wasn't there to see?

All that talk with strange words! Just Valley tricks, not a word of truth in the whole of it. It would be the same way if the Masons got into a Valley court. A Valley lawyer would twist the hard facts just the way Donovan twisted them and let the Masons come back smarter than ever. If Donovan was so smart, let him find that half-moon heelprint and let him—

Wait! How did Corbett know about the bull's-eye lantern?

Stewart stopped thinking and strode across the patch to reach the open barn door. He eased inside, soundless as a weasel after a fat hen. At the far side of the last pile of cured hay, Nelda squatted on a stool, her blonde head pillowed against the cow's flank, milk squirting into the pail as she pulled on the teats.

You got to *pull* milk from a cow, Stewart thought slyly.

The cow heard Stewart and turned to look. Nelda didn't hear and Stewart didn't say he was here.

Squatting there, Nelda sure looked pretty, her short dress baring a knee and the thigh jiggling. What's under that thin dress, only a shift? Stewart wondered. Serves John right to get kilt an' he run off to the woods and don't tend what was his.

The back of Stewart's neck prickled. He stood tense as a hickory board.

When Nelda finished the milking, Stewart had almost forgotten the errand that had fetched him into the barn.

Nelda said, "You are a good bossy," and patted the cow. "Tomorrow morning I come again."

She picked up the pail and rose from the stool.

"I want words," Stewart said suddenly.

The pail banged against Nelda's knee, and some of the milk spilled.

"Stewart, you give me a start!"

"Ain't all I aim to give." He fidgeted, remembering the clean, smooth run of her bare leg. "That day I find our men an' come home, Donovan was in my house, but you don't remember to stop my blabmouth, Nelda."

"Are you here to pick a fight with me?" Her eyes grew big with puzzlement. "The very day your father and John was buried, you want to quarrel?"

"Gran stopped my talk."

"Is there anything in the Hill code that keeps a man from speaking the truth, Stewart?" Nelda set the pail down. "Isn't it your duty to tell Donovan all you know?"

"That ain't our way."

"What is your way?"

"To settle our own wrongs."

"Is that smart, Stewart?"

"Hill smart. Another thing I don't like. How does Donovan know John went off with a lantern?"

"John did carry one."

"You don't have to blab that to Donovan."

Nelda stood straight and pretty, her cheeks the color of wild roses. Sweat dotted her forehead and dampened the dress under her arms.

"Stewart," she said earnestly, "I think you are wrong not to let Sergeant Donovan handle the murders. This isn't the Valley against the Hill, but what is best for us. If I find out anything, I'll tell Donovan. I want that killer found and punished."

"It was *one* killer?"

"So Donovan said."

Stewart eyed her secretively.

"If you know more than Donovan does," Nelda pleaded, "it is smart to speak out. Tell me, Stewart."

"You'd only run to Donovan, Nelda."

"You stubborn Yeoman!"

Nelda picked up the pail. She swayed to Stewart and peered up at his solemn face.

"Why do you act like John when you are Stewart?"

She stood very close. Again his tongue was tied into knots.

"Stewart dear, we need you. Nothing must happen to you. Gran needs you. The sons need you. If anything happens to you, do you want us to starve?"

He could not meet her blue-eyed stare.

"Damnit," he said, staring at her shoes, "don't plague my mind no more. You got to listen to me an' do what's best. At the buryin', you stand with eyes dry."

"I did?"

"You don't cry for folks to see your sorrow."

"Stewart, did you shed tears?"

"A man is different. It ain't right for a new widow not to show sorrow. Gran cried."

"I'm not Gran."

"You best be like her, an' not blab to Valley men!"

"If I do?"

"Then I got to settle you good."

"How will you settle me?"

"Well—"

Always, he was indecisive under her questioning. His eyes worked up the tight dress until he saw the firm lift of her breasts.

Nelda whispered: "How will you settle me good?"

His heart hammered with love for her.

"Stewart dear, I think you are the finest man I ever knew." She sighed. "You will always fend for Gran and the sons. Please, don't ever be angry with me. I am soft and lonely, hardly know where to turn. Will you do something for me?"

Nelda smiled.

"Close your eyes and make a wish! Like you used to wish on a full moon!"

His eyes closed.

"Make a wish, the closest to your heart!"

He thought: She is the prettiest flower on the Hill an' she is John's no more. It is too soon after the buryin' to speak of love, but I wish to marry Nelda Starr.

Light as feathers, her lips kissed the point of his chin. He opened his eyes. Nelda slipped past him and hurried off. Outside, her quick steps faded.

Damn, she sure was a puzzlin' woman!

Why had she made him wish?

Every time she talked he got all mixed up in his mind. Must be her Valley ways to twist things. Sure was different in the Valley. If a man had his troubles, he ran right to the troopers.

Why didn't Valley men stand on their own two feet and meet whatever came along?

He remembered Nelda's fleeting kiss.

Bet her lips are sweet as crushed strawberries in the hot sun, he thought. The next time, you tell Nelda your love and—

Next time?

Four Mason skunks to catch and kill.

That's for tomorrow, he promised.

CHAPTER TEN

IT WAS AFTER EIGHT O'CLOCK and a light wind walked the lake's surface. Beyond gunshot, black duck floated. A brace of wood duck quested a cove. A belted kingfisher rattled harshly over the shallows and winged to a dead tree, where it perched until breakfast swam past. At the shore, a striped snake sunned on a rock. Dotted with blackberry canes and steeplebush, a meadow lazed upward to where Stewart hid.

Lying prone under a covert of laurel, Stewart waited patiently for signs of life within the ramshackle clapboarded house. He knew full well how risky it was to be here. So quietly had he lain for three hours that a male towhee in the glade at his heels scratched and whistled liquidly.

A door creaked inside the house.

"Turn out, ye lazy bastards!" Big Ace Mason roared. "Jeff, outa your dirty nest!" Another door slammed. "Darl! By God, 'tis past time to eat!"

Steps echoed through the house.

"Elly, where are ye?"

Wide of shoulder, Big Ace stepped into the back-yard filth.

"Elly, you to the backhouse?"

Nobody answered.

"You to the barn?"

A rooster crowed.

"Christamighty, where you at?"

Big Ace wet down the back yard.

"That Elly," he grumbled, "is sixteen years old an' don't have the gumption of a pullet. By God, she better quit this woods rovin' or I tan her behind."

Big Ace buttoned his pants.

"Elly! You come arunnin'!"

The order raced through the trees, smacked into the slope, and echoed back.

Stewart thought: I'd gun Big Ace from here an' he so careless, but I need the proof.

Big Ace promised, "You'll git hell when you come home," and stomped inside.

A minute passed.

Behind Stewart, a squirrel chirred in anger. In the woods, the squirrel is a tattletale.

Careful to make no sound, Stewart screwed his body around and lifted his head to see what had upset the squirrel. The laurel lay above the glade and Stewart parted ferns. At the far side, something drew his attention, and he lowered his head until only his cap and eyes showed. Stealthy movement rippled tall laurel and a young girl stepped into the glade.

Elly Mason, truant from the house, had flowing black hair with two freshly picked arbutus blooms tucked over one ear. She wore a short, plain dress with a low neckline and no sleeves. Every bit of skin that showed was tanned rich as walnut stain. In each hand she carried a sprig of dogwood and she walked barefoot. She was a pretty girl with mischievous blue eyes, red lips, and a full-blown body that swelled the dress.

Stewart knew Elly well.

Often they had met in the woods, where she seemed like some sly elfin creature that had sprung from the leaves. A dozen times Elly had followed him, and once had not stopped until Stewart had reached the Yeoman barn.

Elly spotted the male towhee, standing with head cocked. She whistled softly, *Tow-wee, tow-wee, tow-weet.* The deceived male answered. It hopped toward Elly. When it was halfway across the glade, the squirrel chirred again. With a flirt of tail, the startled towhee winged into the middle of a rattlesnake fern.

Stewart thought: She is a child, like a fawn.

Eyes brimming with mischief, Elly mocked the chattering squirrel. It answered back. Elly's rapid chirr tempted it into the glade, its back arched like a cat's and its brush lifted. When the squirrel spotted Elly, it whisked into the laurel.

Laughing, Elly pranced lightly toward the center of the glade. As each knee lifted high, the tight dress rode up the opposite leg. Her hips swayed smoothly and her arms swung rhythmically. Stopping, she faced the laurel where Stewart lay hidden. The dogwood slipped from her fingers. Elly took a slow, deep breath that swelled the dress. Suddenly she lifted the skirt to her thighs and began to dance around the glade's perimeter.

See more of her, Stewart thought, than I do of dress.

Elly floated to a stop. Rising on tiptoes, she swayed back and forth, sending arch glances toward Stewart's hiding spot. She began to sing softly:

> "Oh, I am a merry, merry lass,
> And roam the wood an' hill.
> I am a merry, merry lass
> And wander where I will."

Elly stretched her hands parallel to the ground. When she sang again, she seemed to plead.

> "Oh, that my heart was not so wild,
> My hand and heart so free!

I crave to stay at home and have
A handsome Hill man marry me!"

Her voice was sweet, the tune and words her own.

Laughing silently, Elly ran straight for Stewart, stopped a dozen feet away, and pirouetted gaily.

She don't see you, Stewart thought.

With no warning, Elly stooped and grasped the dress by the hem. She lifted it in a single fluid movement and her hands did not stop until they extended above her head. In her hands Elly waved the dress she had peeled upward off her body. When Elly rose on tiptoes, she closed her eyes and let the dress flutter to the ground. As she poised motionless, not a stitch of clothes on her tanned body, she seemed like some youthful wild-woods nymph who had risen from the soil.

Stewart's breathing stopped.

Elly danced off in utter ecstasy. As she circled, the dance gradually became more untamed. She swooped low until her long black hair trailed on the ground. She leaped like a startled doe. Swoop followed leap in endless, practiced succession.

Now she began to spin, rising first on one tiptoe, then on the other, like an exercise in ballet. Black hair whipped around to cover, then uncover her tense face. Standing in one spot, she spun like a top. Sweat beaded her tanned body. Faster and faster she spun.

With no warning, Elly toppled to the ground and lay supine. Her breasts heaved from the exertion.

She be a child no more, Stewart thought, but a woman.

When Elly sat erect, she crossed her legs and bent her head. The wealth of black hair hid her body from Stewart. Through the hair emerged a low, sweet song.

"Morning is here and I'm alone.
Where is a Hill man just for me?
Oh, that he'd come and love me true,
Carry me off and set me free!"

Blue eyes peeped through the parted hair.

Stewart lay still, as if dead.

With a flirt of her head, Elly whipped the hair over her shoulders. She hummed: "My handsome Hill man—is he afraid?"

Stewart's hands closed into fists.

Picking up a sprig of dogwood, Elly kissed each of the four white banners that formed a single bloom.

"So pretty, pretty," she murmured. "Here I sit waiting, waiting! Where is my handsome Hill man? Why don't he come? Must I sit here and die?"

From down below, Big Ace roared: "Goddamnit, Elly! Where the hell be ye?"

Elly frowned.

"You in that glade agin?"

Elly jumped up in alarm. Stewart flattened behind the fern.

"Big, ugly brother," Elly mocked. "I bet you don't whop me this mornin'!"

Big Ace hollered: "Elly!"

"Cook your own victuals," the girl mocked.

Grabbing up her dress, she scampered across the glade on cat feet and slid through the laurel.

Stewart swiveled away from the glade and stared below to see what danger Big Ace posed. No Mason was in sight.

At the far side of the glade, the laurel parted cautiously. Elly peeped through and stared fixedly at the exact spot where Stewart lay. Her lips pouted.

She whispered, "I love him and he must be stone," and her disappointed face merged with the laurel.

At the west end of the house, a porch leaned at a crazy angle. It held a bench and chair with a faded canvas seat where an old dog slept. Under a basswood tree, three old cars rusted. Swearing voices sounded inside the house.

This is like hunting, Stewart thought. You sit tight and bide your time. In this man hunt, you got to get inside that dirty nest and ferret. You find shells to match the empty in your pocket. You find a boot with a half-moon heel plate and two nail holes. Then you know for sure the Masons killed your kin.

A minute snailed past.

Built like a spider, Old Man Mason slouched from the house and stood on the porch. He scratched his backside, then spat a stream of tobacco juice over the railing. When he yawned, his spider's belly jiggled. Grabbing the dog by one ear, he heaved it off the porch. It whimpered. Old Man Mason said, "Lazy dog, that is my sleepin' chair," and he sat down, tilted back, and hoisted his bare feet to the railing. Settling a hat across his face, he folded his hands across his fat belly and went to sleep.

Another minute passed.

Big Ace exploded.

"Goddamnit, how many times have I got to order ye? Jeff and Darl! You are the laziest half men on this hill. Hustle your draggin' feet. By God, if you aim to eat your victuals here, you spade that patch and scratch in seed."

The Weasel sneaked to the porch. He carried a shiny .35 rifle. A rusty rake leaned against the clapboards and the Weasel picked it up as if it were a rattlesnake.

"What's the sense to plant seed?" he whined. "We ain't never raised only weeds in that danged patch."

Big Ace filled the door with six feet of muscle and beef. He cuffed the Weasel smartly.

"Get to work, you lazy little bastard! Don't stop till that patch be spaded!"

Weasel scurried off.

Lean, wiry Darl, wide and muscular through the shoulders, lean as a whippet at the hips, strolled to the porch. He was the fighting Mason, afraid of nothing.

Darl drawled, "Once this be free hill an' a man his own boss," and picked up a shovel.

"Get a move on," Big Ace ordered.

"What for?"

"I say to dig!"

"Let's see you make me," Darl challenged.

"By God, I can!"

"When?"

The Weasel called, "Let's see you make him," and Darl added, "I am waitin'."

Big Ace knotted his hands into brawny fists. When he made no further move, Darl laughed.

"I ain't the little Weasel," he bragged, "an' you know it. Raise a fist at me and this shovel splits your skull."

Big Ace stood still.

Darl strolled over to the Weasel.

Big Ace snapped at the old man: "Ain't no cause for you to sleep." He spilled his father to the porch floor. As he stepped off the porch, Big Ace tripped over the old dog. He booted hard and the dog limped off.

"Like to see you boot me," Darl said. "That dog was mine an' I would split your skull."

Big Ace ripped off an oath. Hunching his shoulders, he shambled along the grassy lane toward the main road.

He may head for Sloatsburg, Stewart thought. Maybe he goes to seek poor Elly.

This morning there seemed no chance to ferret in the Mason house. Yet if Stewart could snake into the woods and fire a shot, that would fetch the Masons running to see who trespassed and leave the house free for a search.

"We plant seed," the Weasel grumbled, "and the seed sprouts. What happens? A deer eats our work."

Darl laughed and spaded dirt. The Weasel leaned on the rake. Darl stopped and leaned on the shovel.

Old Man Mason roused from the porch floor and hollered: "You lazy sonsabitches! Get to work!"

"You waked us," the Weasel complained. "If you was wuth a tinker's damn, you'd spade the patch."

Darl drawled: "I don't have to do what I don't want to do."

"Me neither," the Weasel agreed.

"Free hill, ain't it?"

"You said a mouthful."

"Get to work!" Old Man Mason jawed, and spat more tobacco juice. "If you plan to eat here, you got to work for it."

"That's the rule?" Darl asked.

"Sure is."

"Guess you don't get no more free food for your spider's belly. You ain't worked for years." Darl pawed at some loose dirt. "Night crawlers. Never seen 'em so fat."

"I don't got to work," the Weasel bragged. "Not so long as I can hunt here and thieve in the Valley."

With that, he broke the rake handle across a knee and flung the pieces toward the lake. He picked up the new rifle.

"I go hunt and to hell with Big Ace. An' don't nobody tell me I *got* to hunt, neither."

"Don't you dare hunt," Old Man Mason warned. "Them goddanged troopers crawl the Hill like snakes and they come runnin' if they hear one shot. They been here twice askin' their damn-fool questions about who bothered to gun a pair of wuthless Yeomans. They don't get nothin' outa me, by God! I don't kill them Yeomans, they ain't wuth it!"

"Ain't no Yeoman wuth his salt," the Weasel sneered. "Just Stewart left, an' he's a piddler."

"I don't have Yeomans on my place, never," Old Man Mason jawed. "Last fall, that no-good John sniffed around Elly an' I run him off with a shotgun. Ain't never been a good Yeoman, 'cept he's covered with six feet o' dirt."

Stewart thought: The old man goes, too.

Darl bragged: "It was me what run John off."

The Weasel said: "I don't care how many troopers is on the Hill," and he swaggered to the lake. Darl watched. The Weasel popped a pebble into a mat of lily pads. Fish jaws snapped.

"That was what?" Darl asked.

"Piddlin' trout."

"Any bass?"

"Ain't the season to fish bass, Corbett says."

"Any bass?" Darl growled.

"Plenty somewhere else. What about a pan fry?"

Darl dropped the shovel. "I'll wet a line. Corbett tries to stop me an' he gets tossed in the lake." Darl entered the house and returned with an expensive rod.

"Where'd you get that?" Old Man Mason wanted to know.

"A Valley man laid it down." Darl laid a hat over the old man's face. "Hold down that chair, Pop. What you don't see you don't blab to Big Ace."

Darl headed east, the Weasel west along the lake.

Stewart rose to his knees.

If the Weasel goes that way, Stewart figured, he may hit into a side trail where I can jump him.

When the Weasel, turned left, dawdling along, Stewart backed from the laurel and stretched hours of waiting from his body. He eyed the spot where Elly had lain.

Sure was fun to watch her dance, he thought. She is light on her toes, like thistle in the breeze. Maybe she dances here to ease that hell-life from her mind.

Leaving the glade, he stalked off. Two hundred yards later, a hollow lazed past a stone outcropping, and beyond that a knob barred the way to the trail the Weasel had entered. Stewart slid around a stand of spruce. Downhill, there was no trace of the Weasel and his rifle.

Behind Stewart the spruce parted and Elly peered brightly at Stewart's broad back.

Since I saw you first, she thought sadly, I loved you. I followed you to the woods and trailed you home. You are not like your brother John an' that is why I love you so. You always spoke kindly. You don't follow me and try to rip the dress off my back, like John did.

A shadow crossed her face.

Stewart, your men are dead an' you are sad. Why do you hide on Mason land and spy? I saw you in the laurel, but you don't know that. It was for you I danced! Why don't you come to me and I was so lonely?

Her nose wrinkled.

"Stewart," she whispered to his back, "why do you carry a rifle and sneak behind trees and rocks? Do you stalk the Weasel? He is quick, Stewart! I am afraid for you. The Weasel will kill you with that gun and your body will rot in a bury hole, like John's."

Elly disappeared.

Stewart loped through the hollow.

CHAPTER ELEVEN

O N THE KNOB, Stewart knew that the Weasel had not passed here. He walked downward to a level place.

Wild flowers bloomed under two huge white oaks, monsters that had withstood the batterings of a thousand gales. At the far side, a white pine that black bears had clawed shaded a tremendous flat rock that formed the top of a ledge. Below, water curled through tumbled rocks and brook music filtered upward.

Stewart selected the oak nearer the trail, and, laying his rifle down, waited immobile against the bole.

Always the skilled predator, he let his mind center on the job of ambushing the Weasel and became all trained ears. Untroubled, the minutes trickled past.

Where was the Weasel?

Why don't he come?

Faint sound floated up the deer trail, a rhythmic, hollow *ka-thump, ka-thump.*

The Weasel spooked deer!

Stewart listened.

Three deer the Weasel spooked.

Louder and nearer, *ka-thump, ka-thump.*

Then *click-click-click,* rattled off.

That was the dry rapping of antlers on dead branches. A buck and two does were headed this way.

The thumping slackened and died.

Stealthily a tremendous rack loomed over the trail. A thick, tawny neck pushed into Stewart's view. Brow points broken off, a magnificent buck stopped.

When its nostrils quivered, it scented Stewart's foreign presence. It was galvanized into action. Taking three monstrous leaps, the buck crashed into the brush, white tail flag lifted.

After an interval, gentle steps strayed in. Two does stopped and lifted oversized ears. Slowly the ears turned toward Stewart. Big eyes studied him curiously and knew he wasn't the oak. As if they had all day, the does trotted off.

That was the way of deer. If there was sudden trouble, the buck thought of number one and left like a streak, but the does took more time.

Stewart listened intently for the approach of the Weasel, who had spooked the deer. How far back was the Weasel? Stewart strained his ears.

Make some sound, Weasel!

An overpowering impulse to peek around the oak tempted Stewart. Just a quick look-see! He fought down the impulse. Long experience on the trail under the old man's patient guidance had taught him never to move while in ambush, not even wink an eye or rub against a tree. So he waited and his impatience mounted with each passing second. Statuesque he stood, pressed closely against the bark, his thoughts busy.

Weasel, whisper some sound!

The sun is to your back and casts your shadow forward.

Where is the warning sound?

Weasel, you ain't a buck on velvet feet. You ain't an owl on silent wings. You are a man an' a man makes sound.

There!

Where there had been nothing on the trail a second previously, the shadow of a man's cap and head burgeoned on the ground. Imperceptibly, shoulders followed the head forward. Below the shoulders poked the lean shadow of a rifle barrel.

With no more sound than that of a strip of cloth waving in the wind, the Weasel edged into sight. Head thrust forward, the left ear cocked, thin shoulders hunched, the Weasel inventoried the sweep of woods ahead.

Around the Mason house, the Weasel might be a setting man, no ambition in his body. Once in the woods, he changed. Here was a deadly man who might sit motionless for hours, then leap into smooth, rapid action within a split second. Here was a deadly man to bait a woods trap and let the old man and John walk right into a blast of Double-O-Buck.

The Weasel's nose quivered.

Stewart took two feathery steps.

In that instant, as if he had the intuition of a buck for danger, the Weasel turned his head and saw Stewart rushing in. The Weasel shifted his feet and swung his shoulders around. The rifle lifted, and in the silence the thumbed safety snicked. As Stewart's left hand pawed the barrel aside, a shot roared out. Smoke spurted from the barrel. Before the Weasel could duck, Stewart's shoulders struck. His running weight rode the Weasel backward.

The Weasel grunted, "Skulker," and dropped the rifle.

He tugged out a hunting knife. Stewart's left hand grabbed the Weasel's knife wrist. His chin rammed against the Weasel's back and he smelled the skunk odor of the dirty man. His right arm slid over the Weasel's shoulder and his wrist jammed against the Weasel's throat. He smashed the Weasel to the ground and tightened his arm.

Like a cornered animal, the Weasel kicked and snarled and clawed with a free hand. Sharp fingernails raked Stewart's cheek and drew blood. Stewart held on. Under him, the Weasel relaxed. The hunting knife slipped from his numbed fingers. Keeping his forearm tight against the Weasel's throat, Stewart shifted to his knees. The Weasel kicked savagely. Stewart shook him.

"Hold still," he warned, "or I bust a neckbone. By God, you ain't the one in ambush."

The Weasel's face turned purple.

"Bragged I was a piddler, eh? Squirm, little Weasel. You are fast in a Yeoman trap."

Satisfied that the fight had drained from the Weasel, Stewart stood and set the half-choked man on his feet.

"You run," he said grimly, "an' I jump you hard." Stewart kicked the knife aside and flung the rifle away. "Weasel, be you ready to talk?"

The Weasel inhaled raggedly. Fingers massaged his bruised neck. A tongue snaked out to lick pale lips.

"Ain't done—nothin' wrong," the Weasel stammered. "Spooked three deer, is all. That ain't cause to jump a man. I only come here after the buck."

"The other day, two Yeomans died in the woods. What about that bushwhackin'?"

"I know naught. Troopers come and that's what we tole 'em." The Weasel's eyes bugged in fear. "Stewart, we be friends. Don't kill me."

"You talk, first. If you don't—" Stewart stuck a fist in the Weasel's face. "Don't give out no Mason lies. Afore I found my kin dead, you bragged in Nauright's Inn you knew a big black thing happened in the woods. You kilt Yeomans?"

"No!"

"I spot your runnin' tracks uptrail to Yell Hollow. Big Ace and Darl run with you. I spot your downtrail tracks, too. That was the day you bushwhacked Yeomans."

"Warn't that way, Stewart!"

"What way was it?"

The Weasel gulped. "Stewart, it was at twilight. We set home all day. We hear three shots from Half Moon Mountain way and that is our huntin' grounds. It is a pump-gun talkin' on our land." The Weasel shivered. "Don't kill me!"

"Keep talkin'."

"Well, Big Ace and Darl and me, we grabbed up guns and run like hell up the trail. I tell truth this time! We run clean to the fork into Yell Hollow. On that trail, we keep to one side an' don't make our tracks. Stewart, I don't hate Yeomans!"

"What lie is next?"

"We see a buck's antlers over the trail!"

"And?"

"We see your old man and John on our land! They still bleed a little, like they just died!"

"Weasel," Stewart warned, "you git one more chance to speak the truth. You bushwhacked the old man and John. Tell it that way."

The Weasel snarled: "Jump the crazy bastard!" His eyes darted past Stewart.

Stewart laughed. "I don't fall for that trick."

Elly Mason said: "Don't hurt him."

At that, Stewart jumped sideways and turned.

By his rifle on the grass, Elly stood by the oak. Wide-eyed, she was like a startled fawn.

"Don't hurt him," Elly begged.

It wasn't Elly that rooted Stewart.

Beyond the oak, Darl Mason lounged, a grin on his scarred face. Darl carried no gun, but at the head of the trail Big Ace waited with a rifle.

"Don't budge, boy," Big Ace ordered, and he strolled forward. "You move a finger an' the rifle talks."

"Stewart," Elly said softly, "I don't want bad fightin'. I saw you hide on Mason land and that's why I fetched my brothers."

Behind Stewart, a breech opened and snapped shut.

The Weasel snarled: "I kill him!"

"Ain't the time for guns," Darl drawled.

"He gits hit in the back!"

"Stop the nonsense," Big Ace ordered. "Twenty-'leven troopers is on the Hill. This is gonna be quick an' quiet. We caught a Yeoman with a rifle on Mason land."

"The bastard near kilt me!" the Weasel raged.

"Please don't hurt Stewart," Elly pleaded. "You promised not to hurt him."

"Shut your mouth," Big Ace said, and lowered the rifle until the muzzle looked at Stewart's belly. He was a hulk of ugly man with fang teeth, loose lips, and beetled brow.

"We Masons," he told Stewart scornfully, "don't mess on Yeoman land. I'll tell you a thing or two, boy. Your old man was a dirty, thievin', trespassin', lyin' old bugger! Your brother was a cheatin', diddlin', braggin' sonuvabitch! He is married but he has to sniff after Elly! Ain't never been a good Yeoman 'cept he rotted in a bury hole!"

Big Ace spat tobacco juice on Stewart's jacket.

"You are a boy and wet the bed anights. You are a doe and no horns on your head. You are a Yeoman skunk an' stink. I'll tell you more, boy. The Weasel told you truth an' Masons don't lie. Yeomans sneaked on our land an' killed a buck. We run up to see what's what. A cute bastard had gunned 'em afore we got there an' saved us the trouble."

"A fact," Darl agreed.

"Stewart," Elly said nervously, "my brothers don't lie this time. The day your kin was bushwhacked they set on the front porch and don't run off till the shots come."

Stewart had to believe pretty Elly.

"Now," Big Ace decided, "we ain't got all day an' tomorrow. You ready, Darl?"

"Always ready for a fight."

"You kill him with your hands."

Stewart asked: "This is to be fair?"

"Sure," Darl said.

"No others buttin' in?"

"That's my Mason word."

"What rules?"

"Hill rules, boy."

"That means no knives," Big Ace said. "Boy, shed your'n."

Stewart shed his coat and knife.

You can't lick Darl, he thought. Run for it. They don't dare shoot an' fetch troopers.

While he knew that he could outrun the Masons, he stood fast. Leisurely Darl unbuttoned his coat.

For miles around, everybody knew Darl's reputation. Darl had bested a dozen tough battlers. One night Darl walked into Nauright's Inn and cleaned out the bar.

Stewart remembered something: When you checked the Masons' tracks to and from Yell Hollow, why did you find no half-moon heel plate?

Belatedly he cursed himself for the oversight that had put him in this pickle. Masons had not bushwhacked Yeomans.

Run like hell, he thought.

It was too late. Darl advanced.

"Cut him to bits," the Weasel snarled.

Big Ace advised: "Groin him."

"Don't hurt him," Elly pleaded.

Quick as a rutting buck, Darl raced in and launched a savage kick. Stewart stepped backward in time. Waist-high, he reached out and grabbed Darl's boot and twisted. Darl rolled over with the twist. He landed upside down and jerked his foot loose from Stewart's grip. Stewart advanced cautiously. Darl whipped over. Braced on hands and feet, he launched a second kick. The boot cracked Stewart's kneecap and he halted. Darl jumped to his feet. He swarmed in like a cat and drove a fist to Stewart's jaw. Stewart swung and missed. He limped because of the kick on the kneecap.

Craftily Darl circled.

When the lithe man with the wide shoulders saw an opening, he stepped in and jabbed a fist over Stewart's careless guard. The fist clobbered Stewart's left eye. Darl back off and waited. Stewart moved in. Darl weaved, straightened, and smashed Stewart's eye with another hard left. Blindly Stewart charged.

Darl slipped aside and stuck out a boot. Stewart tripped and fell. Darl dropped on Stewart's back and rode Stewart flat.

The Weasel shrilled: "Gouge him!"

It was Hill rules.

From the rear, dirty thumbs pressed against Stewart's eyeballs and the thumbs sought for the exact spots to jump the eyes from the sockets. Desperate to escape, Stewart tore one of Darl's hands loose. Reaching backward, he grabbed an ear. With handholds on Darl's hand and ear, Stewart heaved. Darl sailed overhead. Stewart lunged for the rolling man, but Darl escaped.

Sure of his young strength, Stewart lunged again. His hands closed on Darl. They wrapped arms around each other and hugged like bears. They strained and grunted, rolled and hugged, kicked and tried to bite. Finally Darl butted Stewart and rolled free. The men climbed to their feet.

For ten seconds they stood and glared.

Then, hating each other, they ran together with a terrific shock. Darl's fingers fastened to Stewart's throat. As his breath was shut off, Stewart braced with feet widespread. He grabbed handfuls of greasy black hair and jerked backward. Darl screamed.

Big Ace thundered: "That ain't fair, boy!"

"Knock him down an' bust his leg!" the Weasel shouted. "Then kick his face off!"

They were two strong men. Rapt in the struggle, they stood toe to toe and hammered each other. Hard fists splatted on sweating flesh. Their breaths came and went in great, ragged gasps.

Splat, again and again.

Then Darl stopped slugging and returned to a former tactic. Stepping in lightly, he bloodied Stewart's nose with a left jab.

"That's it!" the Weasel encouraged.

Elly moaned, "Please stop it," and Big Ace growled, "Shut your crybaby mouth."

Again and again the long, hard left peppered Stewart's face until his cheeks were pieces of raw meat. Blood salted his tongue. Through split lips, he spat blood.

Darl side-stepped and jabbed, his fist beating a tattoo on Stewart's face. Occasionally he varied the attack with a right hand to the belly. Stewart hesitated. He peered drunkenly from one eye. Darl laughed.

Big Ace said, "You ain't marked him enough," and the Weasel shrilled, "Kill him quick."

A hoop tightened around Stewart's chest.

This ain't the way to whop him, he thought. You got to get in close and use your strength.

Confidently Darl circled.

When he bored in, Stewart leaned backward. The left fist barely touched his chin. He pawed Darl's fist aside. With sheer strength, he waded forward. His left hand fastened to Darl's right wrist. He drove a hard right to Darl's face. In close, another right jarred Darl to the heels. When a final right landed on Darl's windpipe, a hurt look overspread his face. He stumbled backward and broke Stewart's grip on his wrist. In the brief second of respite that he had gained, Darl drew a knife.

Stewart stopped.

"Hill—rules," Stewart panted.

Darl snarled and stabbed with the knife. Stewart leaned to the right. The point of the knife sliced into the loose fold of his work shirt. Before Darl could twist the knife free, Stewart pinned his wrist.

Slowly, inexorably, Stewart lifted. The knife hand was waist-high. Darl braced. He could not match Stewart's strength.

Stewart twisted and rammed his buttocks against Darl's belly. Using Darl's right arm as a lever, Stewart lowered his shoulders and heaved, retaining his grip on the wrist.

It was brutal.

As Darl whirled up and over Stewart's back, a bone in his wrist snapped. Darl screamed. He landed on his back, the top of his head toward Stewart. He lay like a sack of wet sand and his great strength leaked from his body.

"Hill—rules," Stewart panted.

In that moment of exultant, unexpected victory, Stewart had eyes only for the fighter he had licked. As he waded forward, he did not see the Weasel drive in from the rear, nor did he expect interference until the Weasel's arms wound around his knees. Stewart stopped. He reached down to loosen the Weasel's grip. Then Big Ace loomed.

"Got you," Big Ace growled, and swung the rifle. Stewart ducked. The rifle butt cracked against his skull.

"That ain't fair!" Elly shrieked.

Blindly Stewart pitched forward.

"Settles one more Yeoman," Big Ace bragged.

The Weasel yelled: "Darl, you all right?"

"Gonna kill him," Darl mumbled brokenly.

"For God's sake," Elly pleaded, "no more fightin'! Big Ace, no more!"

"Shut your hollerin' mouth," Big Ace ordered. "You are a Mason. Weasel, we don't let it get around this boy licked Darl. We got to figure a way to close his mouth."

Dazed, Stewart rested on the ground.

Took three Masons to beat you, he thought, head areel. You won a fair fight.

He moved his arms until his palms flattened on the ground. With what was left of his failing strength, he pushed upward. His shoulders began to lift, but his chin sagged against his chest. Slowly and painfully, like an old man with gout, he managed to place one knee under his body. As he prepared for the final attempt to rise, a boot crashed against his ribs. Shock knifed into his brain. He fell sideways and lay still.

"I got the bastard," Weasel crowed.

"We will roll him over the ledge," Big Ace decided. "They don't find him for a month o' Sundays."

"Gonna kill him," Darl mumbled.

Elly said: "You don't dare, not with troopers around!"

"He goes over," the Weasel agreed.

Hands tumbled Stewart over and over. When the flat rock was under his belly, the hands stopped their work.

"You hear me?" Elly shrilled. "You push him more an' I will fetch the troopers!"

The Weasel snarled: "Drop that rifle, you little bitch."

"I will fire!"

"Gonna kill him," Darl intoned.

"I git that little bitch to home," Big Ace promised, "an' I strap her till she bleeds. Over he goes."

A kick nudged Stewart's feet over the edge. His knees started to follow his feet.

Teetering precariously on the edge, Stewart made one last, pitiful attempt to save himself from falling. His clawing hands found a wide crack in the rock's surface. His fingers held on. For a moment his fingers braked his slipping body. Then a boot tromped on his fingers and his handhold loosened.

Elly sobbed, "Damn ye," and a rifle roared.

Stewart slid off the ledge. Part way down, his body struck a second ledge and slowed. The rocks jumped to meet him.

CHAPTER TWELVE

NOTHING DISTURBED THE MONOTONY of the black night until a voice urged: "Stewart, try to sit up."

Inside his throbbing head, a rocket exploded and blazed off.

"Stewart, try again."

When he moved, a knife stabbed his chest.

"Wait," the voice said.

Water sloshed on his face. After more sloshing, the shock cleared his feverish brain. He opened his eyes and blinked at the strong sunlight. He lay with his feet in the brook, a rock against his chest.

Elly asked anxiously: "You feel some better?"

A tight rope seemed to bind his chest. When he tried to breathe deeply, a knife stabbed.

"Seems like I fell," Stewart mumbled.

"They pushed you over the ledge."

Facts began to come back to him.

"Elly, was there—a fight?"

"You licked Darl, remember? Big Ace clubbed you."

"Where be he?"

"I drove 'em off with your rifle," Elly explained. "Stewart, it's over a mile to your place. Will you try to stand?"

When Elly knelt over him, she seemed to have the fragrance of arbutus. He remembered, then, that she had danced naked in the glade above the Mason house. In her dark hair she still wore a wilted piece of arbutus.

"Elly," he mumbled, "you are sweet."

"I am?"

"Very sweet."

"Stewart, I love you!"

"You—mustn't."

She kissed his bruised face tenderly.

"I love you, love you!"

"Elly, I got to git home."

"I'm strong an' I will help you."

Her arms slipped under his armpits.

"When I lift, darling, you try to stand. Ready?"

The slightest exertion fetched back the stabbing knife in his chest. When Elly lifted, he worked his muscles, and somehow stood on his feet.

"Lean hard on me," Elly said. "Now take a step."

One foot moved. He plunged into swirling darkness.

"Stewart, can you see?"

The night was black.

"Another step!"

His legs were sticks.

"That's better. Keep walkin'."

Time drifted past.

"Here on the smooth trail," Elly said, "it is easier. You do fine, my handsome man. Step, step."

He seemed to wade in deep water that tried to drag him under.

"Stewart, can you crawl?"

"Crawl?"

Somebody laughed brokenly.

"Stewart, why do you laugh?"

It was the pain inside his head.

Around him, a void tumbled endlessly. A black horse galloped past, stumbled, and plunged to the ground.

A voice wailed: "My God, what happened?"

"I licked Darl," Stewart mumbled.

"What did they do to him?" Nelda cried.

Elly said: "Nelda, take his other arm."

"His face!"

Stewart plummeted into a deep well....

Inch by inch, he climbed up the well toward daylight that was a round hole overhead.

"What's wrong with him?" Nelda asked.

"Well," Doc Painter said, "he's got three, maybe four broken ribs. His face looks as if somebody pushed it into a threshing machine, but that will heal. It's that lump on his head that worries me. Does he keep losing consciousness?"

"Yes."

"Keep him quiet, understand?"

A mist closed inside Stewart's mind.

In the deep night, a star winked on, then another, until the sky filled with stars. When the moon rose, the lonely night changed to silver. The sky whirled, faster and faster.

Stewart took off effortlessly and rose like a hawk to soar in the whirling sky. He winged past a star, swung around the shining disk of the moon, and drifted.

Pretty soon the old man flew in.

"Boy, I don't rest in my bury hole."

The old man flew off and John floated up.

"Boy, soon you'll be on your own two feet again. Take care of the sons, I ask. Nelda is all your'n and you waited four long years for her. Hell, I never loved her nohow. Boy, why ain't you found and killed that smart bastard what bushwhacked us? You know him well an' he is—"

A wind rose and swept John off.

"Come back!" Stewart yelled.

A weight on his chest pinned him down.

"Stewart dear," a voice urged, "don't try to move."

Stewart winged off.

Through a cloud, Gran stepped.

"Boy, I got nobody to fend for me. All my men is dead an' I am too old to live."

Gran faded into nothing.

Stewart heard the murmur of running water.

Stirring, he opened his eyes and blinked in the strong sunlight. At a window where the breeze bellied the curtain inward, he saw the slanted rays of the sun.

This is home?

There stood the familiar kitchen table and cookstove, the fireplace and benches.

Nobody to home?

A thin sheet covered his body. Around his chest he sensed constriction. Lifting the sheet, he saw neat layers of tape around his chest.

"Bed ain't no place for a Hill man," he muttered, "an' the sun still shines."

With an effort he swung both feet to the puncheon floor, and saw that he had slept naked. Waves of nausea worked into his mind. Presently some strength flowed into his numbed legs. He saw more clearly. On the wall, his rifle rested on pegs. Facts returned.

Masons, he remembered. I got to kill 'em all to once or one by one.

He stood erect by gripping the wall bunk. When he started for the rifle, he realized he could not make it and veered to a stop by the side wall. On either side of the cracked mirror he braced his hands. A bloodshot eye stared back at him owlishly. A puffy, discolored lid hid the left eye. A beard blackened his face.

"Masons sure fixed you good," he muttered.

Weaving to a bench, he plopped down.

Well, wasn't much sense to go after the Mason tribe. They ain't the bushwhackers. Proof was what Elly said. More proof was the absence of a half-moon heelprint among the Masons' tracks.

Outside, Nelda laughed.

Then who bushwhacked John and the old man?

"My pretty blossom," Caleb Hall said, "I done all the chores for you again. Anything else?"

"Wood for the cookstove, Caleb dear."

"I'll tote the biggest armful man ever lugged."

Stewart rose and tottered to the wall bunk, where he hid his nakedness under the sheet.

The door opened.

"Sssshh," Nelda warned. "He sleeps."

"Maybe he is dead," Caleb said.

"Don't say that!"

Stewart wondered: How long asleep?

"I'll lift the wood down," Nelda said.

Stewart opened his good eye.

By the woodbox, Nelda took maple chunks from Caleb's arms and laid each one down gently. When the job was finished, Nelda said: "Thank you kindly, Caleb dear. You are the strongest man."

"You are my pretty blossom."

Caleb dear, my pretty blossom!

What happened an' you slept?

Nelda's step neared, followed by Caleb's.

"The ugly bugger needs a shave," Caleb drawled.

"Sssshh!"

"Heard a fact down to Tamburn's store. The Weasel beat this piddler in a fair fight."

"It wasn't that way at all," Nelda said. "Stewart licked Darl, but Big Ace clubbed him and Masons tumbled Stewart off a ledge."

"Like hell this piddler licked Darl."

"Elly saw the fight."

"I don't believe what Elly said." Caleb snorted.

Stewart stirred.

"You'd best go," Nelda urged nervously.

"Hell, he's been like dead for three days. Can I walk you along the road tonight?"

"I must stay here."

"The night is pretty. I aim to pick a handful of stars and tuck 'em in your hair."

"Caleb dear, please go!"

"Meet me at the spring tomorrow?"

"Yes, yes!"

Caleb left.

Stewart wondered: What's atween them?

A cold cloth touched his eyes. When the cloth warmed, a cold one replaced it.

"Get well, Stewart dear," Nelda whispered.

Caleb dear, too.

Nelda toweled his face dry, pulled the sheet down, and washed his arms. She washed and toweled above the layers of tape. When she washed below the tape, her fingers excited his manhood.

Nelda gasped, "Look at him stir," and the thin sheet settled over his body.

"Say something," Nelda pleaded.

Stewart croaked: "Water."

"Praise God, he's alive!"

She pattered off, hurried back with a dipper of water. She helped him sit erect. The spring water tasted good and he gulped greedily, then lay back.

"Caleb was in here?" he asked.

"He helped with the chores."

"You called him Caleb dear."

"You must feel much better."

"What's atween him an' you?"

Nelda sat on the edge of the bed.

"Elly told me that you were wrong to suspicion her brothers," Nelda began. "It was foolish, but brave, for you to go after them alone. That's over. Now—remember I said I'd do anything to find the one who bushwhacked? I meant that, anything! About Caleb Hall and me—the morning after the men went off hunting, we three were at the spring. We did not know our men had been bushwhacked. For no reason as I could see, Caleb said three times he had been to the Valley the night before. Later I remembered that. Why had Caleb kept saying that he was in the Valley? Did he have something to hide? And why did he return to that dirty old cabin? What is in his mind?"

"You think Caleb bushwhacked?"

"I don't know! If he's at the bottom of this or has a finger in the pie, I plan to find out."

"How?"

"I plan to—well, tease him."

"That's why you called him Caleb dear?"

"Of course." Nelda fingered Stewart's arm. "When Caleb trusts me, he will speak his true thoughts."

Stewart thought hard.

With one harsh, final sentence, he eliminated the possibility of Caleb as the bushwhacker.

"You suspicion wrong, 'cause that dumb Valley man ain't got the woods skill to trap an' bushwhack two Yeomans." Stewart closed his good eye. "Nelda, it's some'un else, a man with the feet of a buck. I'll find that man, too."

"Stewart dear, you must rest."

Stewart dear, Caleb dear.

Is Nelda a two-headed woman?

CHAPTER THIRTEEN

T HIS GOLDEN DAY, Nelda warned, "Stewart, you don't have the strength to dig the patch and I will do it," but Gran whined, "Get on with the diggin', boy. We can't sup on wind puddin'."

Stewart wheeled cow dung and covered the patch. Next he plunged the shovel in blade-deep. This was a thing he loved, to work the earth, so rich it seemed alive. Clods crumbled and spilled fat worms. This was his earth, to raise a bumper crop for hungry Yeoman bellies.

As he sweated and dug, a cardinal whistled from the orchard. He paused and eyed the upturned earth.

There was the thrust of Lonesome Ridge, the weathered buildings, and the green saucer of the meadow. Over there, smoke plumed from the Hall chimney. As if he owned Nelda, Caleb had said, "My pretty blossom," and as if she loved him Nelda had answered, "Caleb dear."

How far does a woman go to tease a man and get him to speak his true thoughts?

Stewart scowled.

Caleb wasn't a bushwhacker, but what was in his mind? Now that John was dead, did Caleb plan to spark and marry Nelda?

Never that!

His muscles ached. "You are weak," he muttered.

He remembered a lost fawn he'd once found, and, boy-like, toted home and raised from a bottle. All one summer he and the fawn had ranged far. Come one sudden frosty night in late September and the fawn had run off, never to return.

What happened to it?

He did not know, but he felt somewhat like that fawn he'd carried home. Instead of resting longer, he began to dig. It was monotonous. Push with one foot, lift, and flirt wrists to spill the black dirt. A catbird winged in and stole a worm.

"I got plenty to spare," Stewart said.

Push, lift, flirt, over and over.

When Sergeant Donovan headed upslope, Stewart pretended not to see him until Donovan said: "Morning, Stewart."

"You walk with no sound," Stewart approved slyly. "It ain't mornin' rightly, but past noonout time."

"How do you feel?"

"I don't bellyache."

"Mind if I talk?"

"Go right ahead. You catch the killer yet?"

"If you Hill men would talk, I'd catch him. Three times I questioned the Masons and each time they shut up like clams." Donovan mopped his hot face. "Sure is hot in this uniform. Stewart, why did the Mason brothers try to kill you?"

"They didn't."

"That's not what rumor says. If you sign a complaint against Jeff Mason, I'll catch that killer."

"What kind of complaint?"

"We'll make the charge assault with intent to kill. Once I have the Weasel in a cell, he'll break down and tell all he knows. Will you sign a complaint, Stewart?"

"Can't," Stewart said. "The Weasel is a piddler."

"What's that got to do with it?"

"If I charged the Weasel, folks'd say I was a piddler."

Donovan studied Stewart's impassive face. "Because of the bushwhacking, did you have trouble with the Mason brothers?"

"We had a difference of opinion."

Donovan urged: "Will you sign the complaint?"

"Can't," Stewart repeated. "Lately I had lotsa time to think. I don't want no more trouble with nobody. I figure what's done is done. A man can't set a tree back on its stump."

"Did the Masons kill your kin?" Donovan asked bluntly.

"Doubt it."

"Did you go after them?"

"Mister," Stewart said, "I figure the murders is like a big fire in the woods. The fire dies an' leaves smoke. The smoke dies an' leaves a stink. Pretty soon the stink is gone and you got nothin'. That's where you an' me stand today."

"On your rifle butt, I saw seven notches." Donovan mopped his face again. "Each notch means a man you killed?"

"Man I miss," Stewart answered.

"You're a sly one." Donovan chuckled. "You and I should be better friends, fellow. You're tough and honest and smart. You act dumb every time I question you, but you don't fool me. Oh—Darl Mason won't forget you broke his wristbone."

"I licked him fair."

"So Elly said. I like that girl. Too bad she has to live in that house. Any idea who killed your kin?"

"None."

He rather liked Donovan, yet he could not bring himself to tell him about the half-moon heel plate.

"Killer has to be a Hill man," Stewart added.

"A man who hated your father and John?"

"Nobody hated my old man."

"John had an enemy, then." Donovan searched Stewart's face. "You're the last male Yeoman, right?"

Stewart nodded.

"This bushwhacker is smart and knows how to handle a gun. He can stalk and lay another ambush—for you."

"Why me?"

"Maybe he plans to wipe out the last male Yeoman. Your brother George is dead, your father and John gone." Donovan started off, stopped to call back: "Take care of yourself, fellow."

"Sure will."

Stewart leaned on the shovel and thought: With you dead, no more male Yeomans?

The look of a hawk sharpened his eyes.

Bushwhacker in the orchard, remember?

Uneasily he peered at the nearby woods. Easy for a bush-whacker to hide there and shoot. He glanced at the sea-green orchard. Easy for a marksman to gun you in the back. His bare chest began to grow goose pimples.

Nelda left the house and waved a greeting, then headed down the meadow path. She wore a new dress.

He sneaked into the woods, trailed the brook downhill, turned upslope, and eased through the thick brush and laurel until he reached the side of Caleb's cabin. Nelda high-stepped through the weeds and paused at the front porch.

She called gaily: "I'm here, Caleb dear."

Wearing Sunday clothes, Caleb joined Nelda.

"My pretty blossom," he said, "you look sweet in that new dress I bought in the Valley. Ain't no Hill nor Valley girl with your looks."

"Really?"

"The fact is, and I didn't tell you before, I always had big eyes for Nelda Starr."

"Why didn't you speak before I married?" Nelda said.

"Well—"

"Bashful man! Do we walk to the Valley?"

"We sure do. I got a pocketful of cash to blow an' you buy any dainties your heart craves. Married to that shiftless John, you never had any dainties."

"That is spilt milk," Nelda said.

"What's the piddler doin'?"

"I told him to spade the patch."

"Work is all that piddler knows." Caleb bulged his muscles. "Someday I aim to tan that piddler's hide. I can bust him with one hand tied."

"Don't forget he licked Darl." Nelda smiled. "I bet you were afraid of John!"

"Me?" Caleb snorted. "I ain't never met the man I can't bug-squash an' I wanted to."

"You hated John?"

"He wasn't worth hate."

"I wonder who killed him," Nelda mused.

"Warden Corbett, an' that's for sure. You ready?"

"I must be home early to tend the sons."

"Let the piddler tend 'em. I will take you to see a moving picture." Tall Caleb stared long at the arcs of flesh above the neckline of Nelda's dress. "By God, you sure are an eyeful!"

Hand in hand, hips rubbing, they walked off.

Stewart thought bitterly: That is just teasin'?

Lollygaggin', that was what the two planned. Caleb would buy her dainties, walk her home under the full moon, stop on the road, an' Nelda would let him...

Stewart strode back to the patch and tried to sweat out his bitterness at the patch. He worked grimly.

Late that night Nelda stole into the silent house.

Stewart heard her pass into the bedroom. When the bedsprings creaked, he swung down to the floor and parted the curtains where the sons slept. They had kicked off the covers and the June night had turned cool. He recovered them.

An odor of perfume, left behind as Nelda had passed through, eddied in the still air.

He muttered bitterly, "Stink water what Caleb bought her," and went to bed.

CHAPTER FOURTEEN

Just as soon as the seeds sprouted to green the patch, Stewart returned to work on the McCaffrey cabin.

Atop the side walls he nailed plates and set rafters, added tie beams, king posts, and struts. This morning he hefted logs to a scaffold to side the open east gable.

Mrs. McCaffrey arrived with a bright "Good morning."

From the scaffold, Stewart grunted.

"Why so grouchy?"

He grumbled, "I got work to do," but the fact was that Nelda had gone with Caleb to the Valley yesterday, the third time.

"Stewart, would you like to work here after the cabin is done?" Mrs. McCaffrey asked.

"That's for Mr. McCaffrey to say."

"Why is it?"

"A man has the say around his place."

"That's the way you run your house?"

"Yes."

"And I thought Nelda had some spunk!" Mrs. McCaffrey laughed. "Lately I've seen her pass with Caleb. Does Nelda have your permission to visit the Valley with him?"

With savage blows, Stewart drove a spike home.

"Caleb Hall," Mrs. McCaffrey purred, "is so big and strong, so much of a man. No wonder Nelda prefers him."

Stewart fitted another log.

"Will Nelda marry him soon, Stewart?"

He worked grimly with the log.

Nimbly Mrs. McCaffrey mounted the low scaffold and stood close to him. "Twice," she began, "I asked you to cut a window space in the north wall. Why didn't you?"

"Wind is too strong there."

"Fiddlesticks to the north wind!" Her hand crept inside his. "How does a Hill woman behave at home?"

"Well, she tidies the house and works the outside chores. She carries water an' tends the sons. What is in the cabin is his, not her'n. He says an' she does."

"You really believe such nonsense, Stewart?"

He said, "Man is boss," repeating his father's teaching.

"Sometimes you talk and act like a child. Good heavens, a Hill woman must be a fool to put up with you!" Her hand tightened on his. "Do you treat a woman like a squaw?"

"Man is born to boss," he repeated.

"But this is the twentieth century, Stewart! A woman has a right to her own opinion! Because Hill men have always treated their women so shabbily is no reason why you should do that, too."

"You don't talk sense," Stewart snapped. "Our way is best an' that's that."

"You're just Hill stubborn." She ran a manicured fingernail down the swell of his bare chest. "Sometimes I suspect you're all Indian. Don't the squaws ever rebel?"

"No!"

"Must you shout?"

"Ain't shoutin'!"

"Why are you so angry?"

"You said *Indian!*"

"Don't you like that word?"

"Ain't much Indian blood in me, but I ain't shamed of what's there!" He tried to stifle his anger. "Once the Delawares owned

Jersey an' this tail end o' York State. They were kings. Up here, a woman don't question a man's mind."

Uneasily, because the ideas were secondhand from his father, he stared downward, wondering if everything his father had said was gospel. His face softened.

"Two fawns there," he said, and pointed.

"Ummm, so pretty. Where is the mother?"

He pointed to the doe, statuesque in the brush.

She asked: "And the father?"

"Guess you don't know a buck's way, ma'am."

"What is his way?"

"Well," Stewart explained, "there is more does than bucks. After the heavy frosts in the fall, a buck gets ruttin' hot an' don't give a damn for nothin' an' that goes for a man, too. He takes any doe what comes along. If they don't come, he seeks 'em. Sure has a time for hisself! Comes November, an' he is skin an' bones. That is a buck's way. When a thing *is,* that makes it best."

"A buck should stick to one doe, like man and wife."

"If you had your way," he said dryly, "there wouldn't be so many fawns each spring."

She asked suddenly: "Are you like a buck?"

"No."

"I satisfy you?"

She was keen for mischief, he noticed.

Often, while he had been ill, he'd thought of this strange, love-starved woman. In his heart he knew it was wrong to tumble her. Because he loved Nelda, he had decided never to touch her again, no matter how much she tempted him.

She leaned hard against him. "Stewart," she whispered, "why do Nelda and Caleb hold hands?"

"Don't know."

"Will they marry soon?"

"Can't say."

"Nelda lets Caleb kiss her!"

"You saw that?" he asked harshly.

"Of course. He took her into the woods, too."

Stewart stood rigidly, his jealousy a mounting flame.

"Are you strong?" she whispered.

"I got logs to fit!"

"Don't be so surly."

He waited.

She whimpered: "Take me like Caleb takes Nelda!"

Madness raged in his mind.

"Stewart, not up here!"

He swept her up and leaped from the scaffold.

Mrs. McCaffrey whispered: "Asleep?"

He lay still, the smell of pine needles around him.

"Stewart, who killed your father and brother?"

"Can't rightly say," he answered, and yawned.

"A Hill man?"

"Has to be."

"Somehow," she said, snuggling closer, "I know you're in grave personal danger. Perhaps this killer plans to wipe out every male Yeoman. What do you know about him?"

"Well, he is woods smart. Moves like a shadow. He is like a buck. Had to be to set an' spring a trap on the old man an' John. Maybe he is too smart. I find his special footprint."

"What was it like?"

Something warned him.

"Well, this man can set still for hours an' not blink an eye. If I find his rifle or shells or that special footprint, I got him."

"Tell me more about the footprint," she urged.

"Guess it ain't important, ma'am."

"It's important to find him before he kills the last male Yeoman! What was special about his footprint?"

"Ain't no cause to worry. I say it's up to Sergeant Dorovan to find the bushwhacker."

"Does he know about this footprint?"

"He checked the ambush spot."

"Promise that you'll be careful, Stewart." She leaned over him. "Nothing must happen to you, understand?"

"I ain't a fool exactly."

"Stewart, may I have a north window in the cabin?"

"You got one big window to the south."

"I want to see in both directions."

"You can't see both ways at once," he answered, and that settled the matter in his own mind.

Later she tiptoed off.

She sure is a spunky woman, he thought. Must be miserable for McCaffrey to take her orders. The way to handle a woman right is to let her know who's the boss, not let her fix fingers to your nose like Nelda does to Caleb an' tug him *her* way. What's Nelda see in that dumb Valley man? He can't find his big feet in the woods. He can't stalk a buck an' fetch meat home. But he's got her! He kissed her an' took her in the woods!

The rasp of the big saw bit into his thoughts.

Rising, he stalked to the cabin door. Inside, Mrs. McCaffrey stood on a box. She was trying to saw the thick logs to make an opening for a north window.

That's a stubborn woman, he thought.

The saw snagged in a crooked groove. "Damn," she snapped.

"Ain't the saw," Stewart said, and she turned.

"Why do you laugh?"

"Fun to watch you bust up this nice cabin."

"It's mine."

"All right, bust it."

She struggled to free the saw. The box teetered. Stewart lifted her to the ground.

"Please, may I have a north window?"

"It's your funeral, ma'am."

She kissed him avidly. "That's for a man who gives in to a woman, Stewart!"

"I got more'n that from you for nothin'."

"We can—"

"Tole you I ain't a buck," he said slyly.

He measured the dimensions of a new window on the side wall, nailed boards outside the vertical lines. "Support so the logs don't tumble out when I saw," he explained. "Support is what a man gives his woman, ma'am." Easily he jerked out the stuck saw. "A man goes right on supportin' his woman an' she does his say." He sawed perfectly down one vertical line. "The trick is to let the weight of the saw do the work, ma'am." As he cut down the opposite line, he pushed the sawed length outside.

"All done," he said, and laid the saw down.

"Stewart, are you still mad at me?"

"What you said riled me some."

"Indian?"

"Not that, ma'am."

"What?"

"You pried."

"Pried?" she echoed, puzzled.

He nodded.

"I shouldn't have asked about the killer?"

He nodded again.

"Stewart, I pried because I worry about your safety!"

"That was your real reason?"

"Of course."

Stewart smiled.

"You think I had a different reason?"

"Yes."

"What?"

"Donovan."

"Can you read my mind?" She pouted. "Very well, Sergeant Donovan came yesterday after you went home. He asked me to question you about the killer because he believes you know something you haven't told him. And you didn't tell him about that special footprint, Stewart. Why don't you tell him?"

"He is a Valley man."

"You don't trust Donovan?"

"Our way, an' it goes 'way back, is not to trust Valley folks. When a man keeps his blabmouth shut, he lives longer. I been wronged an' I don't blab all I know. I set out to mend the wrong." Casually, as if he merely mentioned the time of day, he added: "I got to find that bushwhacker an' kill him."

She protested: "It's wrong to kill!"

"Tell that to the bushwhacker."

"It's still wrong to kill!"

"That is your way an' Donovan's way."

"Stewart, it's the only sensible way! The Hill isn't a pioneer settlement! It's too late for you to follow blindly the teachings of your father! Promise not to seek out this killer!"

"You don't know our code, ma'am." Stewart's chin set stubbornly. "Hill folk look to me to settle the wrong what's been done. Nothin' is to stop me, neither. When I kill him, the Yeoman dead'll rest an' not haunt the lonely nights."

"Do you believe in ghosts?"

Stewart nodded.

"But that's pure superstition!"

"Don't understand that word rightly, but I know ghosts. The one I remember best is the Major."

"Who is he?" she asked curiously.

"Major John André, the British spy what the Continentals hung at Tappan, not far from her in the Valley. One dark, windy night, maybe I meet the Major on the road."

"Don't talk ridiculously!"

"The first George Yeoman seen the Major die. He looked not one bit scared. Funny thing, though. They buried him in his underclothes. Folks that see the Major on the Hill say he seeks his uniform."

After a moment Mrs. McCaffrey asked quietly: "Can you really see into my mind?"

"No."

"How did you know Donovan had asked me to question you?"

"Hell, you kept using the same words he spoke to me, ma'am." Tilting her chin, he said: "You are slim and pretty as a dappled fawn in spring. Your hair is the gold color of the full moon in hottest summer. Your lips is sweet as June strawberries an' you don't tell Donovan what I tole you."

"If I do?"

"You won't."

"What makes you so sure?"

Stewart grinned.

"You are a damned, know-it-all Indian!"

Wisht I could tame Nelda Starr, he thought sadly, the easy way I do this skinny woman.

CHAPTER FIFTEEN

DURING FRIDAY NIGHT, the Yeoman cow got loose from the barn and raided the patch. When Stewart saw the ruined crops, he stormed into the house and told Nelda: "Why didn't you stanchion that cow last night when you milked?"

She stared, astonished. "What happened?"

"The cow et up the patch!"

"But I did stanchion her."

At the cookstove, Gran dropped a dish. "Boy," she said, "that Valley woman don't stanchion the cow."

Nelda said: "You weren't in the barn to see, Gran."

"Know what I know."

"Why didn't you speak up last night?"

"Hit's about time I spoke up," Gran said slyly. "You never done your chores right. You never do work like a Hill woman an' poor John knew that, too."

"I did more than my share for John."

"Lies," Gran snorted, and headed for the patch.

Stewart scowled.

"That sets us back two weeks for food, Nelda. I work from sunup to sunset and you be careless with the cow."

"If the cow got loose," Nelda insisted, "somebody else did it. Gran don't know what she sees. Have you noticed how she's faded?"

"Don't put the blame on Gran."

"I only speak fact, Stewart. Gran's hands shake so she can't hold things. She's broken a dozen dishes."

"I ain't worried about Gran."

"Are you worried about me?" Nelda tossed her head. "We can live in my cabin."

"John's cabin," Stewart corrected. "You do your chores right an' don't wrangle."

"I wrangle?"

It was not the ruined patch that angered Stewart, but Mrs. McCaffrey's tales about Nelda and Caleb Hall.

"Save your questions," Stewart snapped. "By God, I go seed that danged patch."

Outside by the patch, Gran wailed: "Every livin' thing gone. When you learnin' that Valley woman proper?"

"I'll learn her," Stewart promised.

"When?"

"Noonout time, maybe."

"Boy, you whale her backside with a strap." Gran smacked her gums. "She was too high and mighty with John, too. I tole him to strap her good, but he didn't. My man strapped me once an' I didn't forgit *that* in a hurry." Gran ambled to the house. "Right on the bare behind I got it. Ate standin' for a week, too."

Stewart cleaned up the mess. Running new furrows, he planted more seed. "Damn nonsense not to stanchion the cow," he grumbled. "By God, you settle Caleb Hall."

All morning he busied himself with the heavier work, began to saw and split stovewood. Twice he refused to heed Nelda's call to dinner. At two o'clock, tuckered out, he ate cold food in silence. Gran was asleep, Nelda angrily silent, and only the sons frolicked.

"I figure to catch a mess of fish," Stewart decided. "That is, if anybody here has the gumption to pan-fry 'em. By God, I need some fun after all I put up with in this house. Young Tad, you wish to see the lake?"

Tad came running.

"The sons should nap," Nelda said shortly.

"I never napped an' I was a young'un." Stewart swung little Ned to his shoulder. "I never fixed the cow so careless she worked loose an' ruint the patch."

"According to some people," Nelda said coldly, "only a Yeoman is perfect. I stanchioned that cow last night."

"That's right, blame the cow. She unlatched the door, too."

"Stewart, the door was unlatched?"

"Another thing you don't do right."

"Stewart, somebody did spitework."

"You hint it was Gran?"

"No. A cow can't slip a stanchion, unlatch a door from the outside, and head right to the patch. Why didn't the cow head for the meadow grass?"

"Don't burn the house down an' I'm gone," Stewart said, and, carrying little Ned, he gathered his rod and can of worms and followed Tad past the barn.

Peace lay on the Hill.

It was there in the blue arch of sky and the hot sun, in the fully leaved trees, the flood of bird song, and Tad's happy chortlings. When the blue water of the lake gleamed ahead, the sons shouted happily.

"You are fine young'uns," Stewart approved, and set Ned on the wide trail that circled the lake.

Tad showed some of John's wild strain and Ned did what Tad tried, but that was because Nelda didn't train them right. All the sons needed was a man to fetch them up right.

Stewart stuck a forked stick by the shore, baited his hook with a fat worm. If the bass didn't bite, and it was the wrong time of day for bass, then he would settle for a pickerel or some perch. Wetting the line, he laid the pole athwart the forked stick and weighted the butt with a flat stone. He stretched on a dry, flat place where he saw both rod and sons. When Tad wandered too far uptrail, Stewart whistled him back promptly.

"You play here by me," he ordered.

He yawned pleasantly.

It was good to rest after the long week's work at the McCaffrey cabin, plus all the extra work around the Yeoman place. It was past time that things were done right. Might be a fine idea to buy some hens and a rooster, if he could get some cash. Nelda could tend the flocks and trade eggs for staples at Tamburn's store.

"Tad," Stewart said, "you fetch rocks and build a house."

"House," Tad lisped, and hurried off.

The hot sun toasted Stewart's back. Something tugged the line, but he did not notice. He yawned hugely, and had trouble keeping his eyes on the busy sons.

Fun to lie there.

"Waitin' for what?" he muttered.

A quick sleep, maybe.

Hey, a scamper at Red Scomp's tonight.

You don't ask Nelda to go, not while she lollygags with Caleb Hall, he told himself. Maybe she don't plan to go. If she does go, Caleb takes her. Bought her a new dress, didn't he? Caleb will dance with her an' hold her close.

His mind closed. Forget that.

You don't like scampers, he thought, but you go see what's up. Mrs. McCaffrey is goin'. She better lug old McCaffrey with her. Hill men don't waste time and a woman is eager for more than fun. Hill men get danderlion wine or good applejack in their bellies they don't give a hoot what woman struts up and asks for it!

Faintly the noise of the playing sons reached him.

Hot sun sure teases a man to take a nap. Can't work from sunup to sunset, an' then some more, and keep goin'.

They are good sons. Like to own 'em. Like to have *mine* some-day. Nothin' like a houseful of sons to run wild on the Hill. A man lives for his sons. For his good wife, too.

Softly the water lapped on the shore. Nobody stirrin' but the sons. Past four o'clock, too. Leaves stirrin' and—

With a start, Stewart awakened.

Long shadows trailed through the woods. From the middle of the lake sounded a girl's laugh. That was a Valley girl in a canoe with a Valley man.

Stewart called: "Tad?"

An echo drifted back.

"Tad!"

Nobody answered. Stewart whistled.

When he did not hear or see the sons, Stewart's first wild thought was the lake.

He ran along the shore, soaking his shoes, studying the shal-lows, and thinking dread thoughts. When he found no tiny foot-steps along the shore, he sped in the opposite direction. Again he found no prints of the sons in the spongy margin and knew the sons hadn't drowned. Along the trail, he sprinted to where the brook slid into the lake. The sons hadn't crossed the brook. He called, but the sons did not answer. Back he raced to where the trail dipped into a low, wet place. Again, no sign of the sons.

Had they wandered home?

You got 'em pinned down to the woods, he reasoned. They are atween the rill and that wet place.

"Tad, Tad!"

The empty echoes floated back.

A terrible thought jumped into his mind.

While he slept, had that bushwhacker made off with the sons?

"The killer may plan," Donovan had said, "to wipe out all male Yeomans."

"Can't be that bad," he muttered.

Using the trail as a base, he began to lope crosswise between the brook and the low, wet place. Sixty yards from the trail, the ground roughened, the trees thickened, and bushes hindered the quick search. Sweat streamed from his body and his fears mounted. Calling in a low, tense voice, he combed each stand of hucklebush, smashed in and out of laurel thickets, burst headlong through chokecherry, tripped over runner vines, waded into brier tangles. Still he failed to find the sons.

A hundred yards from the lake, the ground was higher.

Storming over a hump, he plunged to the edge of a tangle where a sudden twister had felled a dozen trees two summers back.

In there?

Twilight had deepened. There was scant time to continue the search alone. He strode beside the tangle trying to locate hiding places where the sons might play. Piled rocks loomed ahead. A tiny cave there, remember? Suddenly he stopped.

At the rim of the tumbled rocks, one rock lay horizontally to form the top of a shallow cave. At the mouth, young Tad sprawled in the grass and wild flowers. A yard from Tad, little Ned curled.

Stewart breathed easier.

Just like young feet to stray far. His own always had.

Well, Nelda tole you they needed a nap, he reminded himself. Here they are, safe. When young'uns tire out, they just drop in their tracks an' sleep like the dead. You fool, wasn't no cause to fret! Woods is a safe place for man an' kids. You ought to know that. Hell, you was raised here. Nothin' bad ever happened to you.

As he moved forward, his careless feet rustled the dry leaves and a brittle stick broke with a crackle. Between the sleeping sons, something moved. As if he'd bumped an oak, Stewart stopped.

A fat, sinuous form, a perfect blend with the grass and dead leaves, erected a flat, venomous head over a tightly coiled body. Horny, interlocking joints blurred on the tail.

Rattle-rattle-rattle, the blurring tail warned.

In horror, Stewart froze.

Cold, evil eyes stared up at him. A forked tongue darted every which way. Menacingly the flat head poised to strike. The sound was the worst of all.

A big bastard snake, Stewart thought numbly. Lives in that cave. Stand still, man. You keep quiet and it glides under the flat rock. Let it calm down.

In deep sleep, Tad's bare foot moved.

It wasn't much of a stir, but it drew the attention of the angry timber rattler. The weaving head poised eighteen inches from Tad. Time seemed to stand still. For some inscrutable reason, the snake did not strike. If Tad moved again...

Very carefully Stewart leaned forward. The snake veered to the newest danger. The tail rattled.

Measuring the distance between himself and the snake, Stewart took one slow step and stabbed forward with his lifted right leg. With the speed of lightning, the snake struck at Stewart's leg, a blended movement so fast and deadly there was no time to see the jaws gape, the fangs swing down, and the body uncoil in a length of fat lunging danger. There was just the fraction of a second—Stewart had anticipated the strike—for him to swing his leg aside.

The snake missed the shifted target. It landed and writhed, fangs bared. Before the snake could recoil, Stewart stamped down hard with his lifted leg. His boot pinned the snake at the neck. The thick body lashed. The tail whirred. Saliva drooled from the gaping jaws and venom dripped from the fangs. Young Tad cried out and little Ned awakened.

"Ain't no fear," Stewart said.

Very calmly he drew the hunting knife that was always strapped to his belt. It had a bone handle, a six-inch blade. It was sharp as a razor from constant honing. With one expert slice, Stewart severed the head from the lashing body. Pent breath hissed between his clenched teeth. Kicking the writhing body into the cave, stamping on the snapping head, he grabbed up the sons.

"Ain't nothin' ever to hurt you, not while I am here," he soothed, and strode off.

Darkness settled over the back yard. From the house door Nelda watched Stewart approach, a laughing son on either shoulder.

"It's 'way past their suppertime," she said crossly. "Why did you stay so long?"

Stewart swung Tad to the ground.

"Lake is a nice place to tarry."

"Tad's dirty as a pig!"

"Dirt'll wash off."

Nelda took little Ned.

"He wet hisself! You careless fool, why don't you take better care of my sons?"

"Fetched 'em home safe."

"You can't carry them off to the lake again!" Nelda stared at Stewart's empty hands. "Well, I got hot grease ready for a pan fry. Where are the fish?"

"They don't bite."

"Where's your rod?"

"Left it to the lake."

Nelda jeered: "What else did you do?"

"Killed a snake."

"You want me to fry *snake* for supper?"

Nelda shooed the sons inside and flounced after them. Self-angered words floated outside.

"Dirty as pigs, both of you! He can't take you to the lake again! These—these stubborn Yeomans! He went fishing and killed a snake! What do we eat for supper?"

Humbled, Stewart stepped inside to wash.

Under the sink rested two dip buckets that Nelda had neglected to fill with fresh water. Without thinking, Stewart picked up the pails and headed for the spring.

Right after a cold supper, Stewart left the sound of Nelda and Gran jawing and headed for the barn. Not that there was work to do there, but he tinkered and fussed for an hour, anyway. The cow was safely stanchioned. He shoveled fresh droppings outside, strawed the sow and cow, then leaned against the wall and dawdled over a cigarette. He noted the dwindled hay, mere scatterings left from last summer's ample harvest.

"Guess the cow don't let herself into the patch tonight," he muttered, and ground out the cigarette. He remembered to latch the door from the outside, then waded the starlit back yard and entered the dim room where Gran slept in the barrel chair and the sons were behind the drawn curtains of the wall bunk.

Gran whispered: "That my man come home agin?"

"It's me, Gran."

"John, I'm glad you come here agin!"

John?

"What kept you so long in comin', John?"

The back of Stewart's neck prickled.

"You hear me?"

Stewart stared.

"Float closer," Gran whispered.

Stewart glided forward.

Gran's eyes were closed in sleep.

"Knew my man son 'ud come agin," Gran said. "I want words with you. Things ain't right in this poor house."

Stewart thought: Where's Nelda at?

"Nelda," Gran said. "Your Valley wife lit off agin. Togged out in a new green dress. She wore high heels, too. Thought you ought to know, John. Why does that Valley woman wear high heels?"

Scamper tonight, Stewart thought.

"John, I clean forgot about that. You always liked to dance an' hug the gals. Speak to your Valley wife. Ain't no good cames from wearin' high heels, I say."

A chill ran up Stewart's spine. Silently he prompted: Caleb Hall.

"John, twicet the Halls tried to steal our meadow."

Stewart stared.

"John, put some gumption in the boy. 'Tis past time he found out who kilt you and my man. The boy don't have your git-up-an'-go. He ain't a man yit, not by a barnful."

Stewart backed off.

"John, don't go yit!"

Stewart kept backing off.

"I am lonely as the night wind!"

Stewart reached the door.

"John, come see me tomorrow night."

Stewart whisked outside.

He scratched his face. The skin tickled.

"Sure as hell, you ain't John," he muttered. "How come Gran read your mind?"

He re-entered and stomped his feet to awaken Gran. She awoke with a start.

"Boy, where you been so long?"

"To the barn."

"What kept you?"

"Fussed with the cow."

"That Valley woman leave the cow unstanchioned agin?"

"No, Gran."

"She ruint the patch."

Stewart asked: "Anybody here?"

"That Valley woman run off to the scamper."

"Nobody else here?"

"The sons. Nobody comes to see an old woman, boy." Rising, Gran walked to the warm cookstove. She poured coffee into a cracked cup. At the table, she stirred in sugar with one finger, then licked the finger dry.

"Boy, you head to the scamper?"

"Guess not."

"What you need is a frolic to liven your bones. A man needs some play. You go to the scamper. You are all I got left, 'cept the gran'sons, an' they be the spittin' image o' John, not that Valley woman."

Stewart walked outside.

It was a night washed clean, with the Big Dipper canted in the north sky and the Milky Way a tumbled love walk, and for a moment the moon was snagged to a tree tip. Tree toads piped and a whippoorwill mourned over the meadow.

Faint music rode in from Red Scomp's house, by the north woods. That was Baxter Johnson on the harmonica and Penny Conklin, up from Ladentown, sawing on a three-string fiddle. Soft sounds of stamping feet drifted in and Penny hollering the calls.

"That ain't for you," Stewart said, and let his feet carry him down the Yeoman lane.

CHAPTER SIXTEEN

WEARING SOILED WORK CLOTHES and face unshaved, Stewart hadn't planned to attend the scamper, but wayward feet tugged him toward the music. Mrs. McCaffrey's blue car stood in Red Scomp's lane. Dancing feet grew loud and so did the jig of fiddle, the wheeze of harmonica, and Penny Conklin's calls.

"Keep time with the fiddle,
Swing your lady down the middle!"

To the rousing music, big feet stomped and women squealed.

When Stewart arrived at the fringe of the front yard, the music stopped. A man boomed: "Sing us another, Penny!"

The fiddle started up.

Where the old men gathered in a circle, Sam Kitts swung a bottle and sang off key:

"Apple whisky, that's for me,
I'll drink the stuff till I dee!"

The men chorused, "Till I deeee," and round and round passed the bottle of applejack.

Old Pete Dunn cackled: "Listen to the tale of Ben Wartle. He sparks Rose Melick an' she was watchin' the bull have a time for hisself with the cow. 'By God,' Ben says, 'I'd like to do that!' Rose let on she don't understand an' she says, 'Go right ahead, our cow ain't perticular.' Say, ain't that a great tale?"

Stewart wandered off and stood at the back door. Dancers paraded past. Caleb strutted with Nelda. When they stopped near the door, Nelda saw Stewart and waved. Caleb scowled at Stewart. Nelda looked pretty in the new green dress.

Penny Conklin sang out, "Balance your partners, balance away," and Caleb whirled Nelda off.

Because he was clad in his old clothes, Stewart backed off and stood within a lilac tangle well outside the bright light.

Sure was jam-packed in the house. Nelda passed with Caleb, Mrs. McCaffrey with big Jake Smith.

"Eight hands, and away ye go!"

Stomp, stomp, stomp.

A couple sneaked past Stewart.

"Too hot in there for me," Mrs. Penny Conklin said, and the man said, "It be hotter if Penny catches us," and she said, "If we run off in a hurry Penny don't catch us," and arm in arm they headed for the dark woods.

Penny Conklin hollered: "Promenade, now round ye go!"

Stomp, stomp, stomp.

"Dip for the oyster,
Dip for the clam!
Swoop for the pork chop,
An' swoop for the ham!"

The house shook.

When the music stopped, Nelda slipped into the back yard.

She called softly, "Stewart?" and walked with the green dress lifted high. Because he was unshaved and dirty, Stewart did not answer. "Stewart," Nelda called, "Caleb's gone off and left me," but Stewart kept quiet. When Nelda wandered away, he stood silent and lonely.

Music followed more music.

Mrs. McCaffrey strolled past with big Jake Smith.

"Have you seen Stewart?" she asked Jake.

"Not hide nor hair, ma'am."

Suddenly: "Does he love Nelda?"

"If he don't, the man is crazy."

"It's a good thing Stewart's not around to see Caleb hugging and kissing Nelda!"

"Nelda, she ain't right in the head if she lets that loudmouth do that. Say, you comin' to the woods with me or what?"

"I'm afraid of the dark!"

Jake laughed and carried her off.

Jake is no poke in the mud, Stewart thought. Mrs. McCaffrey best mind her p's and q's.

He waited.

Above the beat of the music, somebody brayed drunkenly: "Hey, Corbett snoops out back!"

With whisky in their bellies, men hollered and ran to the back yard, and women screamed.

Neil Pitt roared: "I got the bastard!"

Crack, and a hard fist smacked against bone.

Men swarmed toward the fight.

Git outa here, Stewart thought. They find you hidin' an' they don't ask if ye be Corbett.

He joined the men ringing the fighters, who rolled and thumped each other.

"That ain't Corbett," a man said, and another warned, "What the hell do we care?"

On top, Neil panted: "I got—the wrong one!"

Everybody heehawed at the mistake. Men slapped their legs. A tall Hill man leaped high, cracked his heels together, and hollered: "I'm a tomcat!"

A woman screeched: "Where is Corbett?"

"Ain't seen him."

"Fight's over," another man yipped, and a woman yelled, "Where's the fiddle music?"

"Balance your partners, balance away!"

The fighters hugged each other and shook hands. Men and several women swigged from bottles and drifted toward the music. Red Scomp spied Stewart.

"Glad you come," Red said. "Nelda allowed you was too tuckered to come. You got a swig bottle?"

"I work tomorrow."

"Hell, this is tonight!"

Red handed over a brown bottle. Stewart took a careful swig. Applejack slid into his belly.

"That stuff sure oils the gut," Red said, and teetered. "Ain't you danced yet?"

"No."

"Nelda, she makes a sweet armful."

Stewart scowled.

"Wisht I warn't married!"

Stewart waited.

"If that gal slept to my house in my bed—"

Stewart's hand closed on Red's shirt. "Watch your dirty tongue," he said thickly.

"Hell, I don't mean nothin'!"

"Say naught agin Nelda."

"She is a good gal."

Stewart's hand loosened.

Red drained the bottle. "You be damn touchy since the day you whopped Darl Mason." Red heaved the bottle into the woods. "You lookin' for trouble?"

"No."

"I ain't scairt." Red grinned. "Brighten up, Stewart. Go swing Nelda."

"Caleb has her."

"Only once or twice. I ain't seen nor heard Caleb's big mouth for a half hour." Red pounded Stewart's back. "I got an idea. We find Caleb and you shut his blabmouth."

A man reeled up and shoved a half-gallon jug under Red's nose. Red lost interest in Caleb. Stewart returned to the front yard, where the old folks mingled and the kids hollered.

Caleb crossed the Scomp patch and stepped into view.

Acts like he owns this place, too, Stewart thought.

At his back, somebody whispered urgently: "I found you!"

Stewart turned.

"Elly Mason! How come you are 'way over here?"

"I had to come!"

"Why?"

"Stewart, we got to get away!"

"What's up?" he wanted to know.

"I can't say it here!" She tugged him along the lane.

Stewart said: "What is the matter?"

Up ahead, Mrs. McCaffrey's blue car loomed.

Elly hissed: "Listen!"

Steps sounded behind the car.

"Who is it?" Stewart whispered.

"Ohmigod," Elly sobbed. "Quick, into the bushes!"

He let her drag him into the thick shadows.

Three men pushed through the starlight and clustered by the blue car. At the sound of the voices, Stewart stiffened, and Elly dragged him deeper into the bushes.

"What is in this car?" the Weasel asked.

"Keep your thievin' hands off," Darl warned drunkenly.

Big Ace hiccuped. "What's here be mine."

"Like hell," Darl said.

Stewart's muscles bulged. "Aimed to catch up with 'em," he muttered. "Ain't no better time."

"Ssshhh," Elly warned, and fingered his lips.

Stewart took a step.

Elly slammed hard against him.

"Why do you think I run here?" she whispered frantically. "At home, they got drunk. I heard them plan to come here and get you." Her body was an urgent plea to stay. "Don't fight them."

He stood uncertainly.

"I find handbag and gloves," Darl drawled. "Like to meet the man says I can't keep 'em."

"I got a flashlight," Big Ace growled.

"I only got cigarettes," the Weasel whined. "By God, I thieve a new tire for my old car."

"Take the wheels an' all," Darl suggested, and Big Ace added, "I git the chance an' I take the McCaffrey woman."

At the house, the music stopped.

"Hide the things," Big Ace ordered. "After the fight, we pick 'em up. You ready, Darl?"

"I been waitin' long for this. Weasel, you got a handgun to hold off the men?"

"Sure."

Elly whispered: "That's why I ran to save you."

Stewart patted her back.

Maybe, he thought, if you let the Masons go ahead, you can jump the Weasel first an' take his gun.

Big Ace said: "Listen!"

At the house, a man began to sing.

That is One-eye Dunn, Stewart thought.

The words of the "Valley Man's Lament" drifted along the lane. One-eye Dunn sang:

"—hoot an' a holler,
A holler an' a hoot,
Valley man don't get rhubarb up."

A dozen voices repeated the refrain.

"Oh, he run for a mile,
He set by the fire,
Valley man don't get rhubarb up."

More voices swelled the refrain.

"Oh, he drank applejack,
An' swilled mountain dew,
He used up the lard
An' all the butter, too!
He rubbed an' he rubbed,
He pounded an' he scrubbed,
But—
Valley man don't get rhubarb up!"

A mighty shout tore the night apart.

Elly pressed against Stewart. His arm tightened around her slim waist.

"Great singin'," Darl applauded.

The Weasel said: "None better'n One-eye."

"Darl," Big Ace ordered, "you take that Yeoman boy this time."

"Come on," Darl growled, and they headed off.

As their steps faded, Elly said bitterly: "And they are my brothers!"

"Don't you mind."

Elly whispered, "Come," and led Stewart along the starry lane. At the curling hill road, she rose on tiptoes and kissed him full and hungrily. Her lips were fresh and sweet.

"I am so sad," Elly whimpered. "Stewart dear, take me from that awful house."

He waited, not knowing what to do.

"Stewart, I saved you from my brothers and fetched you home. They whopped me good for that."

"They are bastards."

"Look." Elly lifted her short skirt and bared slim legs. "See how the strap marked me?"

Scars made her thighs ugly.

"The bastards," Stewart growled.

"My legs ain't pretty any more!"

"Ain't what I think." Her legs held his eyes. "Elly Mason, you are very pretty."

"I am?"

He nodded.

"Stewart, take me away!"

"Can't do that rightly."

"Why not?" She fingered his face. "I love you."

"Elly, you are only sixteen an' don't know your right mind."

"I love you!"

He had no answer.

Elly pouted.

"You are not like some other men on the Hill, Stewart Yeoman. They plague me hard and all they want is *their* fun."

He said humbly: "Elly, I love another."

"Mrs. McCaffrey?"

"Never!"

"Who?"

He stood silent.

"Stewart, you love Nelda Starr?"

He waited.

"Let me see your eyes!"

He bent down.

"You love Nelda Starr." Starlight softened the lovely contours of Elly's face. "She is so lucky." Sadly she fled barefooted along the curling road.

Soon her singing floated back.

"My feet are not so wild,
My hand an' heart so free.
I met a handsome trooper
An' hope he'll marry me!"

Her voice faded. Night noises started up. Heavy in heart, Stewart headed for home.

CHAPTER SEVENTEEN

STARLIGHT AND SOME MOONLIGHT lit the big room. On the table, a dirty cup waited for Nelda's rinse pan in the morning, but no one sat in the barrel chair. Stewart peeked at the sleeping sons.

Where was Nelda—with Caleb?

He stepped into the open door of the old man's room. On the double bed, a homemade quilt covered an empty mattress and pillow.

Gran took a walk?

Near the sink, he noted that the two dip buckets were gone, so Gran must be at the spring.

One bucket, he thought, is too heavy for her.

Outside, he saw the empty meadow below. The backhouse door stood closed.

"Gran?"

No sound there.

Stewart sniffed. The barn door stood ajar.

But you latched that!

He strode to the barn and yanked the door wide open.

"Gran?"

The stench of burned wood rushed out. The cow lowed in alarm and the sow grunted. Stewart stumbled over a body.

"Gran!"

As if asleep, she sprawled with one thin arm outflung. He carried her outside. Her body was light as feathers and her work dress soaking wet. Starlight fingered her pale, peaceful face. Her eyes were closed and her head lolled. A hand grabbed Stewart's heart. He ran to the house and stretched Gran on the old man's bed, fetched a lantern, and checked her breathing.

In death, Gran did not stir.

Numbly he set the lantern on the floor. A sob shivered his great body. Sinking to his knees, he began to massage Gran's cold hands, and he cried like a hurt child.

When his grief ended, he prowled inside the barn, using a bull's-eye lantern to spot the grim details.

Where the scattered hay had lain earlier, there were only sodden ashes. In several places where the fire had taken hold, boards were charred. One streamer of ash led to the stall, and where the cow had struggled frantically to escape fire and smoke, her neck was rubbed sore from the stanchion. The two dip buckets lay empty on the floor. An inch-long candle stood in a pool of blackened water.

After you left for the scamper, he reasoned, a bugger sneaked in here, lit that candle, and heaped the hay around it. That give the bugger time to run far before the fire started. Soon as the hay caught, Gran spotted the fire from the house. She grabbed up the full dip buckets an' run here to douse the fire, save the barn and livestock.

The strain was too great for her frail body?

Her heart had bust?

He did not know.

Inside, he found no clue.

With the bull's-eye lantern darting a spear of light, he worked around the barn, found something at the rear. On hard ground covered with a film of dust, there were several faint steps, like those of a man on tiptoe, pointed at the rear door, seldom used by Yeomans. This rear door stood ajar. Where the runoff from the manure pile had soaked the ground, Stewart saw a man's clear footprint. He studied that print tensely, hardly daring to believe the evidence of his eyes, because this was the telltale print he had sought, a half-moon heel plate with two nail holes.

"The killin' bugger," he growled.

Whoever had bushwhacked the old man and John had dared sneak close and try to harm the Yeomans further. He was a big man, too. Weight sank the footprint deep. It took more than weight to fire the barn. It took a bushwhacker's black heart.

Stewart thought, He be your'n to kill, and wanting no one else to find the trace, he blotted the print out.

"Gran," Stewart said, "that bugger was the cause of your death, too. I will right the wrong that is done us."

At the spring hole in the meadow, he rinsed the stained buckets at the overflow, and, filling them with fresh water, walked sorrowfully to the house.

Night deepened toward early morning.

Outside the house, a quick step sounded on the lane, then Nelda arrived in the big, starlit room. She stepped from the high heels and walked to the wall bunk, carrying the slippers. After she had checked the sleeping sons, she whispered: "Stewart?"

Unseen, he loomed by the fireplace.

Gliding into the middle of the room, Stewart told Nelda's back: "Long past time for you to come home, woman."

Startled, Nelda wheeled.

"Stew-art, you scared me!"

Barefooted, she padded closer. Above her smiling face, her hair was tumbled.

He thought bitterly: She is two-headed.

"Stewart, why did you scare me?"

"You wear a new dress an' high heels!"

"Ssshhh, you'll rouse Gran."

"Wisht to God I roused Gran!" he said fervently. "Where do you git the new clothes?"

"You'll rouse the sons."

"Don't side-step a question." His anger was at the bursting point, but he kept his voice low. "Where do you git money for new clothes?"

"I didn't need money." Nelda swung the slippers idly. "It is nearly sunrise and I won't fight with you. Folks saw you at the scamper. Why didn't you dance with me?"

"I wore old clothes!"

"That's the only reason?"

"Caleb Hall had ye!"

"Goodness sakes alive, you talk as if Caleb owned me. I danced twice with him. If you had stayed, you'd have seen that. After the Masons came, Caleb got drunk and passed out cold."

"You sneak to the woods with him?"

"I did not."

"You got drunk an' he pawed you?"

"Don't you dare think such lies," Nelda said tensely. "If anybody sneaked into the woods, it was you with Elly Mason. Lots of folks saw you walk off with Elly, and did their tongues trumpet at such goings-on!"

"Elly is only a child!" Stewart towered over Nelda. "Where do you git new clothes?"

Nelda sighed.

"Answer!"

"Stewart, I am very tired."

"Where?"

"The new clothes came from the Valley."

"Whose money?"

"If you must pry, Caleb's money."

"Woman," he growled, "if you are to live in this house, then you take no more from that Valley bastard!"

"Who says so?" Nelda challenged.

"I say!"

"You are my boss?"

"I boss my place!"

"You sound the way John used to talk when he was drunk," Nelda mocked. "Stewart dear, please don't be like your brother. Why don't you smile more? Why didn't you dance with me at the scamper?" Nelda sighed. "Sometimes I don't understand your manners. You act like—well, like you hated me! You sound as if a dress and slippers meant I'd done something awful, an' I haven't! What's wrong with a lonely girl having new clothes?"

"New clothes don't make a man an' damn right don't make a woman! You keep clear o' Caleb!"

"You understand this, Stewart Yeoman: I never was John's squaw and I'm not your squaw because I live in this house." Anger hardened her face. "The big mistake I made was being only seventeen, not knowing my own mind, and John sparked and married me because I thought he was a fine man."

"Say naught agin the dead!" Stewart warned.

"The dead?" Nelda laughed. "I speak the truth when I please about John. He cared nothing for me, just wanted two sons, like I was his squaw! John always thought of number one, and nobody else. If he wanted to hunt or fish, he did. If he wanted to sit shiftless, he sat the whole day through, then tomcatted the night. It didn't matter to John that the roof over our heads leaked, that the windows were broken, no wood for the cookstove, and less victuals for our stomachs! All John wanted was a bottle of liquor and time to chase after every woman who—"

"Don't talk agin the dead!"

Nelda's voice sharpened. "I'll say what needs to be said! I spoke my piece to John and I will speak it with him dead! He was no true husband, but a shiftless, lazy, fightin', lyin', chasin' man! The way I hear it, it's great wonder some husband didn't shoot him long ago!"

Her voice rose to a frenzied climax.

"John's dead an' I'm free! I'm glad he's dead!"

Without thought, Stewart slapped her.

Nelda reeled backward, more from the unexpectedness of the slap than from its force.

"Caleb kissed ye!" Stewart raged, beside himself with jealousy. "Caleb tumbled ye!"

Nelda panted: "Who says so?"

"Mrs. McCaffrey saw ye!"

"When?"

"On the Valley road!"

The mask of Nelda's face jerked apart. "She lies!"

"She speaks truth about ye!"

"Don't say that again!"

"She speaks truth about—"

Gliding forward, Nelda raised one slipper to strike.

Stewart tore the slipper from her hand. His great strength ripped off the heel and he hurled the broken shoe away.

"That bastard Caleb!" he snarled.

His madman's hands fastened to the neckline of the new dress. His hands jerked and the fabric ripped down the front. Wearing a white petticoat, and not much else, Nelda stood with shoulders slumped and breasts heaving.

Stewart shivered uncontrollably.

Slowly Nelda's chin lifted.

"The only new dress—I ever had—on the Hill." Tears rolled down her cheeks. "You are just like John. You are a crazy, selfish Yeoman."

He stared, suddenly appalled, at the torn dress.

"Are you satisfied?" Nelda asked.

This wasn't the future he had planned for them.

"I am sorry," he groaned.

She faced him proudly. "Sorry?" she flared.

"Yes."

"That's like spilt milk!"

"Nelda," he stammered, "I—I—"

"You *what?*"

He wanted to speak his love, but his tongue stuck fast and the true words never came.

Nelda snapped: "I'm not satisfied!" Shrugging from the torn dress, she let the garment cascade down her back and drape at her bare feet. "This petticoat is new!" Nelda said. "Why don't you rip that off my back?"

"Done enough to ye."

"Caleb bought it!"

He stood silent, unable to meet the situation.

"Tear it off!" Nelda ordered.

"No."

Nelda stepped free from the dress. Her frenzied hands grasped the petticoat at the top. She ripped the fine fabric and exposed her full breasts.

"This means naught to me!"

She tore the petticoat down the front, slipped her arms from the straps. With a crackle of body electricity, the petticoat slid to the puncheon floor, and Nelda stood proud and naked.

"That rids me of Caleb! Are you satisfied?"

In helpless misery, Stewart closed his eyes.

"I'm through with you, too!"

You love her, he thought. Tell her that.

A door slammed.

When Stewart looked, his bedroom door had closed. A minute passed. The door opened. Nelda walked out wearing a short, faded dress and scuffed shoes.

"The only reason I met Caleb Hall," she said coldly, "was to help you find the bushwhacker before he killed you. If you ever touch me again, I'll split your head with an ax."

Nelda walked toward the wall bunk.

Stewart stammered: "What ye aim to do next?"

"What I please."

"You are leavin'?"

She knew how to hurt him.

"I go to whore in the Valley," she scoffed.

"Nelda, ye can't!"

"Who tells me what to do?"

"Nelda, Gran is dead!"

She turned slowly. "What's that?"

"Gran's dead!"

"She was lively enough at supper to say mean things to me."

"In the old man's room," he said numbly.

Nelda left the big room. When she returned, her step was slow and her face sad.

"Gran never liked me, but I am truly sorry for what I just saw." She stood silent, then: "My mother always said trouble comes in bunches and the Yeomans have had their full share."

He did not answer.

Nelda said quietly: "Gran's dress is soaking wet and smells of smoke. What happened?"

Stewart told the story of the fire, omitted only the telltale footprints.

"If somebody fired that barn," Nelda said, "then that same somebody let the cow into the patch last night."

"I was wrong to blame you," Stewart said humbly.

"What does all this mean?"

"The bugger is close."

"Who is he?"

"I don't know."

Nelda's shoe tapped nervously. "What do you plan to do?"

"Git him."

"So far, you've not done so good."

She had a strong mind, stronger than Stewart realized.

"The thing to do next," Nelda decided, "is for you to take this news to Sergeant Donovan."

"Can't"

"I suppose your stubborn Yeoman mind won't let you do what is sensible. Thank the Lord, I am a Starr and Valley born. That killer has to be caught before he does more harm. I'll go to Donovan."

Nelda started for the door.

"Stay where 'tis safe," Stewart pleaded.

She ordered crisply, "You tend the sons and see what other mischief you can plan for me," and walked into the night.

Miserably Stewart stared at the tom clothes.

You got to do somethin' to win her back, he thought unhappily.

Buy her a new green dress!

Was she safe on the road?

He did not know and dared not think.

CHAPTER EIGHTEEN

AFTER GRAN HAD BEEN BURIED, Sergeant Donovan cornered Stewart.

"By not co-operating with me," he warned grimly, "you've made a big mistake. You haven't given me evidence that you have. What has to happen to make you listen to reason, fellow?"

When Stewart did not answer, Donovan continued.

"You're smart enough to know this bushwhacker won't stop until he's killed you off, too. So far, he's outsmarted both of us. What about telling me what you know?"

Stewart shrugged.

"What about a special footprint?" Donovan prodded.

"That," Stewart said, knowing that Mrs. McCaffrey had run to Donovan with the news.

"What's so special about the print?"

"A half-moon heel plate." The words were dragged off his tongue. "With two nail holes."

"You found that at the ambush?"

"Back of the barn, too."

"A big man's print?"

"Sizable."

"Over two hundred pounds?" Donovan asked.

"He's big. That heel plate ain't on a Hill man's boots."

"What else do you know?"

"That's it, 'cept he moves around like a buck."

"Not much to go on," Donovan mused, "but I'll give it a try." He eyed Stewart grimly. "We're both sitting on a hot griddle, fellow. I've got plenty of pressure on me because I haven't solved the murders. If the killer knocks *you* off—" Donovan shrugged. "Take care of yourself, fellow."

"Aim to."

"Just stay alive," Donovan added, and left.

The lonely days passed.

The pear tree flowered and snowed the back yard with petals. The patch lay untended and the meadow waited.

Twice daily, now that Nelda lived with the sons in John's leaky cabin, Stewart milked the cow and did the woman's chores, but he promised himself, if ever he got married, not to let his wife do such heavy work.

At early morning and twilight, never at the same hour, he left milk at John's porch, along with a pail of fresh water and an armful of cured maple for Nelda's cookstove. Once or twice, when he frolicked with the sons, he saw Nelda, but she did not speak.

As a precaution, Stewart carried the old man's .32 revolver in one hip pocket. Before leaving house or barn, he studied the woods, wondering if the bushwhacker were around. It was not that he lived in terror, but simply that he took no careless chances and set no definite patterns of movement. The odds favored the bushwhacker, who, as long as he continued to remain anonymous, might pick the spot and moment of ambush, as he had done with the old man and John.

When Mrs. McCaffrey sent word up from Tamburn's store that she expected him in the morning, he made the decision to go.

Before dawn he finished the chores. Leaving the usual supplies on John's porch, he slipped into the woods, choosing not to risk the dangerous road. When the sun rose, he arrived at the

McCaffrey cabin, which was unroofed. He began to board the north side.

After noonout spell, Mrs. McCaffrey arrived with a brisk "Can you finish my cabin this week?"

Stewart stood on a scaffold erected by the south side.

"This week, ma'am, I need three days for June hayin'."

"Let that wait. Do you mind if I hire a carpenter from Haverstraw to set the windows and hang the doors?"

"I don't mind, ma'am, but hayin' can't wait."

"Why are you so formal, Stewart?"

"Thought 'twas you, ma'am."

"You're acting exactly the way you did when you first came here to work! Why are you so cold? What makes you so unfriendly?" She edged closer to the scaffold. "Why weren't you at the scamper to dance with me?"

"You had big Jake Smith, ma'am."

Her eyes narrowed.

Before she answered, a rifle cracked. A bullet tore a hole in the roofing at Stewart's right. Mrs. McCaffrey screamed.

A thirty-five talkin' sweet, Stewart thought, and dived from the scaffold.

He shouted, "Run for it," and dodged behind a pine.

A second bullet banged into the pine.

Stewart peered around the bole. Two hundred yards distant to the right, near the top of the south ridge, a puff of smoke lifted lazily from evergreens that topped a rock ledge.

I git him this time, Stewart thought.

As he bolted around the cabin, a third shot spanged into the side wall. He bumped into Mrs. McCaffrey and she gasped: "I'll phone the police!"

"Ain't no need. You got a rifle handy?"

"Don't go after him!"

"Ain't no more danger there than here. You got a rifle here?"

"Yes!"

"Let's get it, ma'am."

With the knoll sheltering them, they reached the house, where Stewart trailed Mrs. McCaffrey into a den. A French door opened on the side lawn. Guns lined the wall.

"My husband is a collector. Take what you need," Mrs. McCaffrey said. "That man tried to kill you! I still think we should phone the police!"

Stewart selected a rifle and found appropriate ammunition in a cabinet. He loaded the rifle quickly.

"You got some Double-O-Buck Remington Express shells in there," he said. "There a shotgun with a pump action, ma'am?"

"No. We had a robbery and the thief stole the pump-gun, a rifle, and ammunition. He also took some of my costume jewelry. Sergeant Donovan thought there was a connection between the robbery and the bushwhacking because the robbery came first."

"Sounds reasonable," Stewart agreed.

"I'll phone the police!"

"I waste time," Stewart said, and, stepping outside, he crossed the lawn and entered the woods.

He knew this territory and his mind worked rapidly.

The thing to do was hit the trail from the main road that passed under the south ridge. That way, he could pin the bush-whacker to the ridge.

At the trail, he kept to the woods and stalked inward. The movement of a bird interested him. The tremble of a leaf drew his attention. Up ahead, by the side of the trail, movement stopped him. His nostrils flared.

Warden Corbett here?

Stalking forward, he ordered: "Don't turn!"

Corbett stood still.

"Drop that handgun," Stewart said.

Corbett dropped his .38 revolver.

"Bushwhacker, you kneel."

Corbett protested: "I didn't fire the three shots!"

"Kneel or git it here."

Corbett knelt on the trail. Stewart recovered the revolver. He examined the soles of Corbett's shoes.

"We take a look at that ambush spot," Stewart said grimly. "You don't wear the half-moon heel plates today."

"Don't be *that* dumb." Corbett rose. "If we go up this trail, it's straight into the bushwhacker's gun."

"You shot and hid the rifle. Move off."

"I hid no rifle!"

"You git it here or up there with your footprints?"

Reluctantly Corbett moved off. Where the rock ledge broke the face of the south ridge, they climbed to the point of ambush behind the evergreen covert.

"From here you fired at me," Stewart said. "If I find your trace, you git it for what you done to me an' my kin."

Confidently Stewart examined the leaves and soft ground. He picked up three empty cartridges. "Shootin' at a man's back," he told Corbett. When there were no prints at the evergreens, he circled slowly, leaned down.

"Damn," Stewart said bitterly, and Corbett bent over a foot-print the killer had left behind.

"Half-moon on a big shoe," Corbett said softly. "So that's the special print the bushwhacker wore, eh?"

Corbett studied Stewart's disappointed face.

"So you thought I fired at you?" Corbett's voice hardened. "Stewart, you're not so smart as you think you are. I'll tell you something you don't know. Sergeant Donovan is convinced the bushwhacker will kill you next and today proves him right. Ever since the fire in your barn, Donovan or I or somebody else has watched you. Nights, we sat outside your house waiting for the bushwhacker to appear. Today I watched with binoculars from this ridge. I heard the three shots, but couldn't pin-point the ambush spot. You found me on the trail because I was after—"

The bugger legs off, Stewart thought, and started west along the ridge.

Corbett called, "You left me unarmed," and Stewart dropped the .38 he had picked up on the trail.

"Two men are better than one," Corbett urged.

The bugger heads west, Stewart thought, to cross the road an' get back to the Hill.

He broke into a fast lope, following the easiest way along the ridge. Five minutes later he had outdistanced Corbett.

Ten minutes later he reached the road. Carefully he checked left and right for a hundred yards, but failed to see where the bushwhacker had crossed.

Across the road, he worked uphill into the deep woods. There was another trail, he knew, that led from the road toward the big lake on the Hill. This was slow, puzzling work, like looking for a pin in the haymow. The circle that he followed fetched him back to the Hill trail, a mile from the big lake.

For minutes, he watched the trail. Nobody passed.

Shrugging, he worked down until the trail was underfoot. This was the ticklish part in the chase. If the bushwhacker had used this trail, he might wait up ahead and gun the first chaser that came along.

It was a chance that Stewart had to take.

With the rifle ready and the safety off, he began to head for the big lake. He moved stealthily, eying each spot of possible ambush, making sure no bushwhacker lurked there. He watched the trail for footprints.

A brook wound in from the left and crossed the trail. For long minutes, Stewart worked the woods. Satisfied finally that the bushwhacker had not chosen this spot for possible ambush, he returned to the trail and moved forward to the crossing.

The bushwhacker had already preceded him.

There was a faint track of the half-moon heelprint on this side of the brook. At the edge of the brook a man had knelt down to drink and left his kneeprints behind. At the opposite side of the brook, six feet distant, the bushwhacker had left a deep heelprint in soft dirt when he had jumped.

Stewart paused. Should he go on?

Can't git him if you stand here, Stewart decided, and leaped the brook.

He was in no hurry. A hunter never hurries.

An hour later he had covered a quarter mile of trail and the big lake was near. From time to time he'd found trace of the bushwhacker, but nothing else.

As the shadows lengthened, he saw where the bushwhacker had left the trail and headed into the thick woods. He followed cautiously.

Ten minutes later, he was licked. The trail had vanished. From these woods, all the bushwhacker had to do was head for the Hill and vanish.

CHAPTER NINETEEN

RIPE MEADOW HAY waits for no laggard.

The next morning Stewart began to mow the meadow. Starting at the spring, he cut several circular swaths, then worked upslope beside the ancient path. From the old man he had learned the patience of scything.

Standing with shoulders slouched and knees slightly bent, he swung the curved blade attached to the end of the crooked handle. It was swing, slide foot, over and over, with an occasional pause to whetstone the blade. The ripe grass dropped evenly. When a frantic pair of meadow larks hovered, Stewart located the nest and left a patch of grass to shade the nestlings.

Morning heat spilled into the cupped meadow. Stripped to the waist, he sweated and brooded.

Late last night Sergeant Donovan had stopped at the house. Neither he nor Corbett nor other troopers who had rushed to the Hill in response to Mrs. McCaffrey's phone call had picked up any more trace of the bushwhacker. "I made a *moulage* of the half-moon heel plate," Donovan had said. "All I need is a pair of boots to match." Donovan had taken the McCaffrey rifle and promised to return it. "I'll keep watch when you mow tomorrow," Donovan had said. "I don't think he'll strike so soon."

Hay don't wait, Stewart thought.

Swish—swish—swish of the scythe, and the grass died so that the cow might live through the zero winter.

Once he rested flat by the spring and gulped mouthfuls of sweet mountain water that bubbled up through the sandy bottom, overflowed, and trickled downslope to keep the meadow green.

Across the calm surface a skate spider fled. A spotted frog stared bug-eyed from the shallows. A newt crawled on the sand. It was frog and newt that cleaned the spring.

The revolver in his hip pocket was heavy. He wrapped his shirt around it and hid it under a rock by the spring.

Back to work, man.

Swish—swish—swish, and the tall timothy toppled. Noon arrived and passed unnoticed.

It took a good man two full days to scythe this meadow, another day to stack and tote the hay barnward in great forkfuls. Three days of killing work, and no time to stop and cook victuals. Then back to the McCaffrey cabin and finish that damn roof. Maybe you get more rifle shots. Maybe you get the shots here.

When movement drew his eye to the lower meadow, he paused. Nelda had left John's cabin and moved with the sons upslope.

There was the hot sun overhead in the sky's great cup; the tall, uncut grass trembling in the light breeze; fork-tailed swallows winging the good air; a bluebird's whistle; a half-naked man resting on a scythe, a blonde woman in a short, tight dress, and two yelling, dark sons—peace on the Hill, haying time in June.

The sons yelled and grabbed Stewart's legs. He patted their heads and Nelda said: "I fetched hot victuals."

While he wolfed food, Nelda walked to the barn and returned with a hay fork.

"Good food an' thank you," Stewart said.

"I ask no thanks," Nelda answered, looking off. "You are in danger each day, but you always cared for the sons and me. It isn't neighborly to see a working man skip his meals."

Idly she forked some flattened grass.

"On the Sloastburg, my father taught—" Nelda paused.

She wore a faded dress, clean and neatly darned. In addition, she wore a single item that Stewart had never seen before. At the hollow where her breasts dipped under the neckline, she had pinned a gold bird with one brightgreen eye.

Watching the pin, Stewart prompted: "What was it your father taught?"

"That cut grass dries better if it's turned over after it lays in the sun several hours." She glanced covertly at Stewart. "That cures the underside. I fetched a fork."

"A man needs help in hayin' time."

"You want me to fork?"

Meadow and house and barn are lonely places, he thought, when she and the sons are off.

Aloud: "A man needs all the help he can get."

"My father was right about turning the hay over?"

"It ain't our way."

Nelda headed for the barn.

Without thinking, Stewart said: "Let the sun shine on both sides of the timothy."

Nelda asked: "So the hay cures faster?"

"Like your father said," he agreed.

Nelda smiled impishly. "I never thought the day would come that a Yeoman changed his stubborn mind!" She began to fork.

The sons frolicked.

Good to have everybody near again, Stewart thought as he mowed. Maybe Nelda has forgotten about the slap and the new dress you tore. She don't wear the one you bought her.

At four o'clock Mrs. McCaffrey arrived in the blue car and walked leisurely down the path. She nodded distantly to Nelda, passed Ned without a glance, and stopped by Stewart.

"After yesterday," she began, "I worried about you. Corbett said you had no luck."

"No luck at all, ma'am."

"When will you finish my cabin?"

"Not before next week, ma'am."

"Today the carpenter arrived from Haverstraw. He can't possibly finish the cabin this week unless you help. If you come tomorrow, I'll pay double wages."

"Hay can't wait, ma'am."

"Don't you need cash?"

"Not so much as the cow needs winter hay."

She stepped closer and her eyes widened. Softly she said, "Why are you so cold toward me?"

Stewart shrugged.

"Don't you love me any more?"

Stewart stared at Nelda's back.

"You love Nelda, is that it?"

He thought: I love Nelda.

"Every man to his own sorrow," Mrs. McCaffrey said. "Of course, she loves Caleb."

"How can I know that, ma'am?"

"It's apparent, isn't it? She kissed him and you know what they did in the woods together!"

He said harshly, "I don't know if you tell the truth," and Nelda turned around.

Mrs. McCaffrey smiled.

"Make a fool of yourself over Nelda if you wish. There's one thing more that will help you judge Nelda correctly. I told you that a thief stole Mr. McCaffrey's guns, that he also took some of

my costume jewelry. You see the pin Nelda wears, a gold pheas-
ant with a green eye? If Nelda is so wonderful, why does she
wear *my* pin?"

Stewart gulped. "You are sure?" he asked thickly.

"I certainly am. The thief stole it."

"Nelda ain't no thief, ma'am!"

"Why does she wear my pin?"

Stewart fidgeted.

"I want my pin back," Mrs. McCaffrey said firmly. "Shall I go
to Sergeant Donovan?"

"You go where you please. Nelda ain't no thief."

She said tartly, "That's for her to prove," and walked off.

Nelda waited by the path. "What lies did you tell Stewart
about me, Mrs. McCaffrey?"

"Step aside," Mrs. McCaffrey snapped.

"Did you say I kissed Caleb on the Valley road?"

"You did more than that."

Nelda said hotly: "You lie!"

She was sweaty and flushed from hard work, her hair awry
and her dress stained.

"Get off this place!" Nelda ordered.

"Do you plan to attack me with that fork?"

Nelda dropped the fork. "I don't need a hay fork to handle a
liar." Nelda took a step, fists clenched.

"You are an ignorant, stupid Hill woman," Mrs. McCaffrey
said coldly, but she walked fast up the path.

When the blue car drove off, Nelda strode to Stewart.

"Why did you tell that skinny woman I wasn't a thief?" she
demanded.

"It's the gold pin you wear."

"What about that?"

"Mrs. McCaffrey said it was stole from her house."

Nelda stared. "Then how did Caleb—"

"Caleb give you that pin?"

"Yes, and two others. He said he'd bought them in the Valley. Is that plain?"

For the first time, everything was plain. Now he understood why Caleb had returned to the Hill. To steal this meadow and get square with the Yeomans. He wanted Nelda, too. That's why he killed the old man and John. He had to break into the McCaffrey house and steal guns and shells.

Stewart's mind worked fast.

Remember how he asked when you'd leave for the woods an' you told him right after dark? Then he got away by sneakin' past your house to home an' come runnin' back with a likely story. It was Caleb that left the scamper and fired the Yeoman barn to kill Gran. Yesterday he hid near the McCaffreys' an' gunned you. That's why his half-moon tracks headed for the big lake an' home. Wait....

"Damn if I see," he muttered, "how that dumb Valley man got the drop on two Yeomans."

Nelda asked anxiously: "You think Caleb is the bushwhacker?"

"Points right at him. He sets right under my 'nose an' I don't figure it's him. How can a dumb Valley man—"

Nelda interrupted: "Caleb isn't dumb! Before he returned to the Hill, he was in the Army for three years. Once he told me about drills at night and how he and the other soldiers learned to crawl silent in the dark woods, not making one sound."

"The bugger!"

"What do you plan to do next?"

Tell her, he thought, an' she runs straight to Donovan.

"Don't know yit," he drawled. "That pin you wear don't *prove* Caleb bushwhacked an' stole. Maybe he did buy the pin in the Valley. Maybe a Valley bugger is to the bottom of this."

"You won't go after him?"

"I think it over first."

"Then you'll go to Sergeant Donovan?"

"Just give me time to think, Nelda."

Nelda urged: "When will you go to Donovan?"

"Right now, there is hay to mow."

"Don't be headstrong!"

Stewart grinned. "Guess I ain't the only headstrong one."

"What do you mean?"

"You sure lit into Mrs. McCaffrey."

"She lied about me, Stewart!"

"You don't kiss Caleb?"

"Not once." As she looked up at him, her blue eyes widened. "I kissed you once."

"On the chin. In the barn." Stewart rubbed his chin thoughtfully. "Well, hay don't let a man stand here an' gab."

From the spring, he began to cut a swath toward the Yeoman line fence. Swish—swish—swish, and the timothy toppled, but he was really scything Caleb's head off. His mind brimmed with Indian cunning. Had to break into that Hall cabin and find the proof. He had to get Caleb off and search that cabin.

Nelda called suddenly: "Where's young Tad?"

Stewart stopped scything. Little Ned rolled near Nelda, but young Tad had disappeared.

"Saw him near the line fence," Stewart said.

"You think he wandered—*there?*"

She meant the Hall place.

"Might have." Caleb was worse than a rattler. "I'll see."

Nelda dropped the hay fork. She picked up little Ned, walked to Stewart, and said hurriedly: "Don't you dare cross that fence!"

"You aim to?"

"I must find Tad!"

He leaned on the scythe, watched Nelda slide through the fence to disappear within the Hall tangle of brush.

Sporadically he cut hay, working nearer to the fence.

It wasn't right for her to go there.

Where was young Tad?

Suddenly he heard distant voices.

He dropped the scythe and crossed the line fence.

CHAPTER TWENTY

FROM A SUMAC SCREEN, Stewart spied on the Hall cabin.

Behind the cabin, out of sight, Nelda laughed.

"Caleb, I'm glad you found young Tad."

Like a shadow, Stewart sneaked to the cabin and entered the open front door. Junk cluttered the main room. To the left, in a small bedroom, there was more litter. In Caleb's bedroom there were blankets on a scabrous iron bed, clothes in a closet, but no shoes with heel plates. Peering into the kitchen, Stewart heard Caleb gabbing with Nelda in the back yard.

You don't have much time, he thought.

Softly he checked the main room.

Nothing in the fireplace, two moldy cupboards, and an ancient hand-hewn chest. That left three places in this room.

In the attic?

Can't risk the ladder now.

Inside the walls?

No time to make noise.

The floor?

He tested the wide floor boards with his feet, seeking a loose board. Nelda, keep Caleb talkin', he begged silently. Back and forth he prowled until only the corner next to the kitchen remained. He lifted a moldy, filthy quilt and laid it aside. A floor board creaked underfoot. A gray maggot scurried into a crack and a fat squish bug—

Fresh saw cut!

Kneeling, he pressed by the cut. A three-foot section teetered on a crossbeam. He lifted the board and laid it aside. Between two joists, inches above the level of dry earth, lay a pair of scuffed boots. Stewart pulled them out.

Nelda called out: "Don't gad off, Tad."

Each heel bore a plate of soft steel, shaped like a half-moon, fastened with two nails. A tick of sound warned Stewart and he swiveled on his knees.

Caleb Hall stood there.

In that instant, Stewart saw the true Caleb.

The huge man's teeth were bared in a silent snarl. His pig's eyes glittered with hate that had never been spoken to Yeomans. His brawny arms were lifted high over his head. He smashed downward with a kitchen chair. Stewart lunged aside in time to escape being brained. The chair glanced off his left arm and shattered on the floor.

Nelda called sharply: "Caleb, what's that?"

In one hand Caleb held part of the chair. The hesitation was enough for Stewart to hurl the shoes into Caleb's face. Caleb stepped back. The shoes clattered to the floor.

From the front yard Sergeant Donovan yelled: "Who the hell's in there?"

Donovan's voice decided Caleb.

He swung the piece of chair at Stewart's face. Stewart drove off his knees. His good arm wrapped itself around Caleb's knees. Splat, and the club smashed onto Stewart's bare back. His hold loosened.

Donovan yelled: "Caleb?"

Caleb slid toward the kitchen. Stewart dived, but missed.

"Stewart!" Donovan panted. "I run here and—"

Pause.

"Whose shoes?" Donovan gasped.

"Caleb's," Stewart growled, and stumbled to his feet, his left arm numb.

"Half-moon—"

Nelda screamed.

Stewart drove through the kitchen, Donovan at his back. They stormed into the back yard.

In her arms, Nelda held little Ned.

"He run off with Tad!"

"Where to?" Stewart roared.

"The laurel!"

A rank, thick patch of laurel bordered the weedy back yard. Stewart drove forward. He hit the laurel with a smash of shoulders, tripped, and sprawled.

Donovan panted, "I'll get him," and crashed past Stewart.

Groggily Stewart rose. He heard Donovan order: "Stop or I shoot!"

Nobody answered.

A gun thundered.

Stewart smashed from the laurel.

Donovan stood with feet widespread. He fired a second time. Thirty yards below, the brook coursed at the base of Lonesome Ridge. On the far slope, Caleb stepped behind hemlock.

"Let's go!" Donovan panted.

He plunged down the slope and splashed through the brook. His foot slipped on a mossed stone and he fell heavily.

"Ankle," Donovan snapped. "Don't go alone!"

Stewart loped up the slope and rounded the hemlock. There was the start of the killing lift to the top of the ridge. There was Caleb, a hundred yards in the lead, scrambling up the slope.

Where's Tad? Stewart thought wildly.

Tad is dead!

Under the hardwoods, Stewart raced through a hollow, climbed the steep side, and pulled himself onto the slope with the aid of a young birch.

Caleb glanced back at his pursuer.

"Come an' git kilt!" Caleb jeered.

"Bushwhacker!" Stewart panted.

Caleb thumbed his nose and went on.

Gradually the trees thinned out. Up ahead Caleb followed the easiest path, as if he knew where he was going or had been here before. For some unapparent reason, Caleb slowed down. Stewart gained and closed the gap to sixty yards.

The crest of Lonesome Ridge rose through the trees. Wolf rocks loomed ominously. Vines and bushes crowded against the rocks. Caleb paused.

"You still coinin'?" he jeered.

"Will chase you to hell!"

There was some reason for Caleb's decision to wait. Stewart slowed to a walk. He advanced cautiously. When he was fifty yards from Caleb, the big man knelt suddenly and reached under a flat rock. He turned.

The rays of the late sun gleamed on the barrel of a shotgun, pump action. Without bothering to stand, Caleb fired.

The second that the shotgun had appeared, Stewart had reacted with the unthinking instinct of a hunter. He dived headforemost for the shelter of a pronged chestnut stump. The open choke pattern of .30-caliber bullets splintered the stump or whistled harmlessly overhead. Gun noise rolled off and echoed back.

Donovan called faintly: "Stewart, wait!"

Stewart reached for the .32 revolver in his hip pocket. His fingers found nothing. Then he remembered that he had wrapped the gun in his shirt and hidden it by the meadow spring.

Warily he peeked around the stump. Caleb had not waited. He stood outlined on the crest.

"You be a dumb Yeoman!" Caleb hollered.

"I don't gun a man in the back!"

Caleb strolled off the crest and disappeared.

Stewart ran to the left of the rocks where Caleb had posed. Low hucklebushes topped the crest. Like a snake, Stewart hunkered down and crawled in. Parting the bushes carefully, he stared below. Off to the right, Caleb waited.

He ain't smart as you, Stewart decided. He ain't up agin the old man an' a reckless fool, neither.

Unarmed, he sought a method to outfox Caleb's shotgun.

A pump-action shotgun holds three shells. Caleb didn't pocket spare shells at the rocks where the shotgun was. The thing to do was to tempt Caleb to empty that pump gun, then jump him.

He studied the slope before him and made a decision.

Inching backward, Stewart regained the slope he had climbed and stood erect. Filling his lungs deeply, he bolted upward. As his shoulders lifted above the hucklebush, he dived headlong. The opposite slope rushed up to meet his belly. He landed with a crash, hands outstretched to break the fall. As he had planned, a rock rose before his eyes.

The pump gun blasted. Splinters of stone whistled past Stewart's ears. Only one shot left in that gun, he thought. The blast rolled off and echoed against the slope like summer thunder.

Stewart yelled: "Come git me!"

"You are a thievin' Yeoman."

"We ain't the thieves!"

"Yah, you stole the Hall meadow."

Stewart bluffed: "I got a handgun. Come git me."

"I fixed two Yeomans an' I'll fix you, too."

"Bushwhacker!"

"Damn good one." Caleb laughed. "Ask John."

"Valley bastard!" Stewart taunted, and popped his head above the rock.

While Stewart had been hidden, Caleb had worked downslope toward the woods, the inner wilderness, and safety.

Stewart rose.

"Fire!" he challenged.

Caleb held the shotgun loosely.

Stewart mocked: "You be scairt to fight like a man!"

"Come here an' see, piddler."

"Am acomin'."

With Caleb in retreat, Stewart's plan changed. His eyes on the shotgun, his body ready to take instant cover, he moved daringly down the slope. At this range, ninety yards, he knew that Caleb must aim the shotgun, not snap-shoot and risk wasting his last shell. The very fact that Caleb did not fire convinced Stewart there was but one shell in the shotgun.

He picked his way carefully, edging more to the right, then downhill. He passed the spot where Caleb had first stood on this side of the crest. He shouted insults to hold Caleb's attention and strolled toward a thicket. Caleb backed into a laurel clump, only his head showing.

Stewart knew this slope like the back of his hand. The moment the thicket hid his stroll, he lowered his shoulders and ran into a familiar hollow that gouged the slope.

Flinging caution to the wind, he raced along the deepening hollow. He ran noiselessly, picking flat spots for his feet, avoiding stones, and keeping his eyes to the left occasionally in case Caleb had moved toward this hollow. A spring bubbled from under a rock and a chipmunk darted under a log. The spring's overflow formed a rill. Under whitewood trees, the hollow widened.

Through this semitwilight, Stewart ghosted silently until he arrived at a point a hundred yards below where Caleb had stopped. Then he climbed from the hollow, and, buck fashion, eased from tree to tree. When he was directly beneath Caleb, Stewart swung upslope to pick a proper ambush.

Using the advantage of every mossed rock, the shield of the slightest depression, the protection of each bush and vine tangle, he worked upward. When a hump of ground almost as tall as a man's head reared itself, he knew that Caleb was not far beyond. This hump was to be the vantage point, where a man might watch and not be seen, where a smart hunter might spring a trap.

Stewart began to crawl the final feet to the hump.

Donovan called from the crest: "Stewart, you fool!"

Pause.

"You—Caleb Hall!"

Donovan's .38 roared. A bullet whined overhead.

"Stand still!" Donovan ordered.

In this lonesome place of danger, the thick-crowned trees shut out the sun. Long shadows hid a crawling man. Quiet as death, the land waited.

Stewart reached the base of the hump. Off to the left, a flicker of brown caught his eye. He flattened and tried to look like a log. A brown thrush lit in a nearby hazel shrub. The thrush whistled once.

Stewart understood that silent movement and whistle. Something had sent it winging ahead. As if in answer to the whistle, a second thrush winged away from the hollow's edge. In low flight, it reached the hazel shrub.

Seconds tiptoed past Stewart's cocked ears.

There!

By the edge of the hollow, bushes parted. Making no sound, Caleb eased into view, his back to Stewart. Shotgun ready, shoulders hunched, Caleb merged with the shadow of a white-wood and peered into the hollow.

He figured too late what you aimed to do, Stewart thought. If you'd run slow down the hollow, the bastard'd have you. He ain't so smart. Everywhere he went, he left the half-moon heel-plate for you to find on the ground.

It was clear how Caleb had outwitted the old man and John. He was woods smart, but not smart enough. He didn't know about the silent, warning way birds fly ahead from danger.

Donovan called again.

Stewart listened to the echoes and decided: Donovan is by the spring in the hollow. If he comes on downhollow, Caleb has to gun him or back this way.

Stewart wormed into a clump of trillium at the base of the hump, flattened, and parted the leaves borne on erect stems. Caleb stood still until Donovan called again. Lightly Caleb backed away from the whitewood.

Caleb thinks you are in the hollow, Stewart exulted. There is a clear way from him to you.

Carefully Stewart closed the whorls of trillium leaves. This was a game he had always loved and often played, but never against a man and that man armed.

Stewart wormed backward, eeled to the right, and placed the hump between himself and the unsuspecting quarry.

His plan was simple. Hide here. Listen for Caleb. With two or three quick steps, jump him from the rear or side.

He hunkered down to wait.

This was the ticklish part of the stem pursuit. The slightest miscalculation of distance and he would get the full blast of Double-O-Buck in the belly. Make his move an instant too soon, send out the slightest whisper of sound, hesitate the littlest…

In silence, time snailed past.

"Patience. Never hurry, boy," the old man had warned a hundred times. "It ain't the fast one what kills the buck. Takes all the patience you got."

From the opposite side of the hump, there reached out a rustle of sound. Stewart rose on hands and knees.

What was that—scratch of pants leg on twig?

Stewart froze.

Whisper of trillium brushed by big foot?

Stewart held his breath.

Caleb backed into sight. Stewart's breath whooshed out. Caleb half turned and spotted Stewart from one eye corner.

Both men froze.

Glittering pig's eyes and predatory hawk's eyes glared across the space of thirty feet. Hate met hate in mid-air, like the crackle of electricity.

Caleb's shoulders twisted and his long arms lifted and his ham hands swung the shotgun around.

Like a fox, Stewart lunged to the right, desperate to erect the hump between himself and death. The shotgun blasted. A hot knife stabbed into Stewart's bare left arm. At the impact of the bullet, he felt no pain. As he rose to his feet, his left arm dangled helplessly. Bright blood ran from the wound and mingled with the sweat and dirt on his body.

Wait for Donovan and his .38?

Call for Donovan?

Stewart thought: Young Tad.

Gathering the last of his great strength, Stewart drove up and over the hump, hurtled down the opposite side. With feet widespread, Caleb waited.

Caleb reared four inches taller, longer in the arms, thicker through the hips. On his massive frame he packed a forty-pound advantage. At sight of Stewart he grinned.

Handling the shotgun like a club, hands around the barrel, Caleb raised it high. Trained to danger, he seemed to move leisurely, but that was pure deception. Measuring the changing distance between himself and Stewart, Caleb waited. As he ran, Stewart seemed to hesitate in stride. Caleb braked the downward smash of the shotgun. Stewart drove hard. With both hands on the shotgun's barrel, with elbows wide, with the butt upraised over his head again, Caleb started a swing to brain the last adult male Yeoman.

Caleb was quick, but not quick enough.

Tight-lipped and merciless, Stewart leaped.

From his knees he started an upward swing of his right hand to beat that smashing stroke with the shotgun. Gleaming in his hand was the hunting knife that he always carried strapped to his belt. It was a good knife with a bone handle. The six-inch blade was honed like a razor's edge.

Stewart's leap carried him under the descending shotgun. The point of the knife stabbed between Caleb's spread arms. Straight and true, at the acme of Stewart's ferocious leap, the point touched Caleb's throat. Stewart's wrist turned over skillfully.

His shoulders slammed against Caleb, who stood rooted like a tree. Blood spurted from Caleb's throat and spattered Stewart. The shock of Stewart's charge, plus the momentum of his run off the hump, rocked the bigger man. Caleb wobbled. Stewart rode him to the ground.

Straddling Caleb, Stewart raised the knife for a second thrust. There was no need to strike again. Caleb sprawled on his back and the knife had already severed the jugular vein. Blood flowed from Caleb's open mouth. He gasped in pain. Slowly a bubble of frothy blood began to form on his slack lips. When the bubble broke, Caleb Hall died.

Suddenly tired, Stewart pushed to his feet. His left arm dangled, but there was no pain. Caleb's blood trickled down his face and dripped to his chest.

He spoke quietly.

"Old man an' John. Gran, you an' young Tad. It is trail's end an' I am a man."

In the silence, a thrush lifted its voice. Clear and sweet, it tolled, *Ee—oo—leeee.*

Stewart shrugged and leaned against a tree.

Belatedly Sergeant Donovan limped up.

He was young, with keen eyes and the jawline of a fighter, but the woods and the trail were not his element. Somewhere on the tortuous route up and over Lonesome Ridge, he had lost his peaked hat, ripped a button off his uniform coat, and stained the sheen of his black puttees.

Stewart drawled: "You are late."

Donovan was a strong man, but the sight of that inanimate thing on the ground blanched his face. "My God," he gasped, and turned away.

Stewart waited.

"All that blood—you're wounded?"

"Sort of a bee sting."

"When did he get you?"

"Last shot you heard."

Donovan examined Stewart's left arm. "The bullet's in the muscle, no bone smashed. I'll rig a sling. Oh—give me that knife."

Without touching the handle, Donovan wrapped the knife in a clean handkerchief and pocketed it. While he readied a sling, an improvisation with a belt, Donovan talked.

"We know Caleb is the bushwhacker, but there will be a lot of red tape before the record is straight. There will be investigations, exhibits to tag, like your knife and the shotgun and so on. The coroner must view the body, the prosecutor and his staff must investigate, and reports must be made. Reporters and photographers will be here. Finally, everything goes to the grand jury."

Stewart wanted to know: "Why all the fuss?"

"It's the law. You'll probably be held on an open charge."

"What's that?"

"Technical—well, possibly on a murder charge."

When Stewart's wounded arm rode in a sling, Donovan asked: "The only weapon you had against the shotgun was your knife?"

Stewart nodded.

"Why did you take the risk?"

"Young Tad."

"What does he have to do with it?"

"Caleb kilt him, too."

"But didn't you hear me yell from the brook? Nelda found young Tad alive in the laurel, where Caleb had dropped him. That's why I tried to stop you."

Stewart gulped.

When the weight had lifted from his mind, he said: "Guess I don't understand *your* law, but this warn't murder. More like killin' a rattler, only a rattler is man enough to give his warnin'." His wounded arm began to throb. He looked Donovan straight in the eye. "It was him or me an' he lost."

Stewart started upslope.

CHAPTER TWENTY-ONE

A s the crow flies, it was fifteen miles from the county jail to the Yeoman home within the Rampart.

"Stewart," Donovan offered, "I'll drive you."

"Thanks, but I got to work that cell outa my mind."

Within the lonely woods, Stewart trailed higher into the Ramapo Mountains. It was rugged land, piled with upended rocks, crisscrossed with ridges, shaded by hardwoods and evergreens, and here and there touched with the coppery glint of sunlit lakes and the music of many brooks.

Home…

Warn't no place like the Hill!

That first George Yeoman knew what he was about to settle here. A man lived good an' he knew how to handle ax and gun, work a spade, wet a line, and pick up a job or two for cash money. What was the tune John used to sing?

> If life was a thing that money 'ud buy,
> The rich 'ud live an' the poor 'ud die.

That made a heap of sense, he thought soberly. Sometimes a man had to dig in and fight tooth and claw to keep what was his.

That cell…

Nine days he had stayed there, like living in a bury box.

"I hold you on a technical charge of murder," the Valley judge had said, "until the investigation is completed and the grand jury sits on the facts."

This morning they let him out and Donovan told about the diary he found in Caleb's cabin.

"A diary," Donovan had explained, "is like the little book that I wrote in. Caleb kept one. He knew that your brother George had been killed in an accident and he returned to the Hill to get the meadow and revenge on all Yeomans. We never did get a chance to find out if he was crazy. One day John bragged to Caleb that he was planning to gun a big buck near Yell Hollow. That was an easy chance for Caleb to set the ambush and make the bushwhacking appear like the work of the Mason brothers. Then Caleb started after you, shooting from the orchard at night, firing the barn that led to your mother's death, and shooting from the south ridge near the McCaffrey's. According to what Caleb wrote in the diary, he wasn't going to stop with your death. His real interest in Nelda was to get close to the sons, whom he planned to kill in order to wipe out the Yeoman name. The grand jury heard all the evidence and they were convinced you were driven to revenge yourself on Caleb. You're free now."

Well, that was the size of it.

When Stewart passed Kanawaukee Lake, the sun was behind the stark thrust of Lonesome Ridge and his stride lengthened. When he turned into the Yeoman lane, there sat John's tumbled cabin with the patched roof that leaked in a rain.

Stewart called out: "Nelda?"

When she did not answer, he peeked into the front room. It was empty and dusty.

Walking up the lane, he thought: Never saw a house so pretty. A man don't need a stone house and gold fish in a pool. Just a sound roof over his head and tight walls. No need for a window in the north side, neither.

New, short grass greened the meadow. Last crop rotted, he thought, because you didn't have time to finish the hayin'.

He entered the empty house. Geraniums bloomed on the window sill and two dip buckets of water stood under the sink. He drank.

Sweet mountain water, none like it anywhere.

Fresh sheet and pillow in the wall bunk?

He stepped outside.

In the well-tended patch, there were rows of string beans and other small vegetables, cabbage plants and tomatoes, ear com standing knee-high, tall poles set for broad beans, and squash vines sending out runners.

Nine days he had been gone!

From the unused shed near the backhouse, he heard a hen cluck. He went there and counted a dozen hens.

The barn door was open.

On velvet feet he entered. The cow saw him. Nelda sat on a low stool and milk squirted into a pail.

Breath held, a lump in his throat, he stood silent.

Nelda wore a faded dress. Her hair was gold and her arms were bare. Good arms, too. Tanned in the sun, strong from work. Good fingers on her hands—calloused.

"That's all for today," Nelda said, and rose.

When she saw Stewart, her eyes widened. "Y-you scairt me!" A smile trembled on her face. "Stewart, it's over and you're free!"

"How'd you know?"

"Sergeant Donovan fetched the news."

"For a Valley man," Stewart said, "he is a fine man."

"Your left arm?"

"About healed." He listened to hen music. "What about the new hens I saw in the shed?"

"My father fetched them. He said we needed eggs and I thought that was proper. Do you mind?"

"Always wanted hens for my place."

"Did you notice the patch, Stewart?"

"Someone spent a lot of muscle an' sweat there. You?"

"Yes."

"Who mowed the hay and stored it here?"

"Red Scomp and Neil Pitt scythed," Nelda explained. "I helped fetch it here." She waited silently for a moment. "Stewart, do you mind that the sons and I moved from the leaky cabin?"

"No."

"Is anything the matter?"

"Everything is good."

Nelda asked anxiously: "What about Darl Mason?"

"Don't plan to fight him."

"Will you fight with—*me?*"

"Had my bellyful o' fightin'."

"I'm glad." Nelda drifted closer, as if someone pushed her. "What do you plan to do next?"

"Well, first I do some of the heavier work here, then I get back to Mrs. McCaffrey's. She sent word I could work there three-four days a week and the cash money'll come in handy."

"And the sons?"

"I fend for them."

She stood very close. Her eyes were blue as a forget-me-not. "What about me?" she whispered.

He stood uncertainly, his tongue tied in knots.

"Before I married John, I knew you loved me."

He blurted: "What's that?"

"Your lips never told me, but your eyes did."

He stood bewildered.

"Stewart, when will you speak?"

All that he wished for stood very near. Gently his arm circled her waist. He tilted her chin and looked into her blue eyes and found his tongue, after four years of hungry silence. In a torrent, all the things he had planned to tell her poured off his lips until they kissed and stood as one.

"I love you, too," Nelda said proudly. "You are different than any man I ever knew."

Swelling his muscles, Stewart said: "Tomorrow we speak to the young preacher an' set the day. I'll ease your hard lot an' I will work from sunup to sunset an' then some more. I will work at the McCaffreys' an'—"

She laid fingers across his lips.

"You'll never work there again, Stewart dear."

"Nelda, it is good cash money."

"If you ever go there again, I'll leave for the Valley!"

It don't make sense, he thought. A man needs *some* cash, an' there was the work. Still, if Nelda don't want that, you better change your mind.

Outside, young Tad yelled.

Stewart said: "Your sons have come, Nelda."

"*Our* sons," she corrected softly, and arm in arm they left the barn.

THE END